She would have stepped away, if that he thought it had gone on long enough, but Hector continued to hold her, as if he was breathing her in, too. As if his feelings were evolving into something that matched her own, something powerful and lasting.

As she finally released her arms from around him, she looked into his eyes, caught an emotion she couldn't quite grasp.

Whatever it was set her heart thumping, her hope soaring, but she was afraid to read too much into it.

Instead, she said, "You have no idea how glad I am that we've become friends."

"Just friends?"

Her eyes widened, and her breath stalled. "Are we becoming more than that?"

"I don't know." He lifted his hand, skimmed his knuckles along her cheek. "I really have no idea what's going on, Samantha."

Dear Reader,

I love creating romances for Silhouette Special Edition, and I love reading them, too. Who can resist a heartwarming story with real-life characters a reader can relate to? But I especially enjoy taking part in a series like THE BABY CHASE.

There are times when writing can be a lonely profession, but working on a six-book continuity allows me the opportunity to be in close contact with the other authors, each one a dedicated professional who has become a friend over the years.

The editors come up with the series idea, the characters and the conflicts. Then it's up to the authors to make those characters come alive, to develop stories that jump off the page and to make sure the subplots line up.

So as you settle into your easy chair and take another trip to Boston's Armstrong Fertility Institute, you'll meet Samantha Keating and Hector Garza. I hope you enjoy their romance as much as I enjoyed writing it.

Happy reading!

Judy

www.JudyDuarte.com

AND BABIES MAKE FIVE

JUDY DUARTE

Silhouette

SPECIAL EDITION

Published by Silhouette Books

America's Publisher of Contemporary Romance

Special thanks and acknowledgment to Judy Duarte for her contribution to The Baby Chase miniseries.

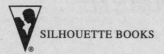 SILHOUETTE BOOKS

Recycling programs for this product may not exist in your area.

ISBN-13: 978-0-373-65524-3

AND BABIES MAKE FIVE

Books by Judy Duarte

JUDY DUARTE

always knew there was a book inside her, but since English was her least favorite subject in school, she never considered herself a writer. An avid reader who enjoys a happy ending, Judy couldn't shake the dream of creating a book of her own.

Her dream became a reality in March of 2002, when Silhouette Special Edition released her first book, *Cowboy Courage.* Since then, she has published more than twenty novels.

Her stories have touched the hearts of readers around the world. And in July of 2005, Judy won the prestigious Readers' Choice Award for *The Rich Man's Son.*

Judy makes her home near the beach in Southern California. When she's not cooped up in her writing cave, she's spending time with her somewhat enormous but delightfully close family.

To the other authors in The Baby Chase series:
Marie Ferrarella, Nancy Robards Thompson,
Susan Crosby, Lois Faye Dyer and Allison Leigh.

Thanks for making this book so much fun to write.

Chapter One

Samantha Keating was on top of the world. Just forty-five minutes earlier, she'd been at her obstetrician's office, on edge and waiting to hear that everything was just as it should be, even though her ever-enlarging baby bump was proof that it was.

She'd been lying on the exam table, her belly exposed and slathered in gel, as Dr. Chance Demetrios ran the ultrasound scanner over her womb.

"Congratulations," he'd said with a grin. "The babies look good, Mom. And we've got at least one boy."

"But are the others doing okay?" she'd asked. "They aren't too small for you to tell?"

Dr. Demetrios had chuckled. "They're the right size, and they've got their fingers and toes, but the other two aren't in a position where I can see the telltale signs."

"It really doesn't matter," she'd said. "I'll love them no matter what."

And now, with the good news still ringing in her ears and in her heart, she couldn't be happier.

Four months ago, at the world-renowned Armstrong Fertility Institute, a leading biotech firm that specialized in areas of infertility and genetic testing, she'd had her procedure done. Dr. Demetrios had transplanted three embryos into her womb, hoping that one would take. It had been so clinical, so unpredictable.

"Now all we have to do is wait," Dr. Demetrios had said afterward.

But Samantha had been too eager to sit around at her mother's house and twiddle her thumbs. So before the clinic could run the official lab work, she'd taken a home pregnancy test and had been thrilled to see the results were positive.

Then, at her first follow-up appointment at the clinic, she'd learned that she was expecting triplets, which was awesome. But it was worrisome, too. There were so many things that could go wrong.

Thank goodness she'd made it through that difficult first trimester. With each month that passed, as the babies grew and developed, she felt more content, more hopeful. And now that she was well into her second trimester and knew that all three babies were healthy and thriving, she could finally relax and enjoy her pregnancy.

And she could finally move back into the house she'd once shared with Peter, the house she'd left after his death. The house that had been a mansion compared to the home in which she'd grown up.

Of course, things would never be the same—and she didn't expect them to be. Her life was about to change dramatically—again—but this time in a wonderful way.

She didn't harbor any unrealistic expectations, though. It would be difficult raising three children alone. She'd realized that going in, and she fully accepted the challenge. This was a choice she'd made five years ago, a decision she would never regret.

A lot of the women who went to the Armstrong Fertility Institute were unable to conceive, but Samantha's circumstances had been different. She hadn't been infertile. Instead, she'd needed medical help to conceive her late husband's babies.

In those dreadful days after Peter had been fatally injured in a tragic car accident, she'd sat at his bedside, grief-stricken and heartbroken, watching a myriad of bleeping machines keep him alive and realizing her hopes and dreams for a family were dying with him.

He'd already made the decision to be a donor, so while plans were being made to harvest his organs for transplant, she'd made a spur-of-the-moment decision to extract his sperm—a secret no one knew, not even her in-laws.

Samantha glanced in the rearview mirror at her smiling reflection, saw the maternal glimmer dancing in her eyes, the healthy glow of pregnancy on her face.

Of course, she realized that there still could be complications up ahead, that the pregnancy was considered high risk, that the babies would probably come early. But Dr. Demetrios didn't foresee any problems at this point, so Samantha refused to dwell on what could go wrong.

Instead, she would focus on eating well, getting her rest and making sure she had plenty of fresh air and sunshine.

Of course, she wouldn't be getting any sunshine today. She glanced at the sky, with its storm clouds growing darker with each city block she passed.

As she neared Primrose Lane, she spotted a moving van turning ahead of her and realized that her furniture would arrive on the tree-lined street just as she did.

She wasn't sure where she'd put the new things, since she'd taken very little with her when she left after the funeral and had gone to stay with her mom. She planned to do a bit of redecorating over the next few months and would probably get rid of more than she kept.

There was a lot to do; she'd locked up the house after Peter's funeral and hadn't been back since. She'd managed to orchestrate all the ongoing maintenance work and landscaping from a distance. And just last week, she'd hired a cleaning crew to get things ready for her return.

All the dishes that had been gathering dust over the years had been washed and put back into the cupboards and on the shelves. Still, she knew there would be a lot of work to do on a home that hadn't been lived in for so long.

At first, she'd stayed away because it had been too painful to be there without Peter. And because she'd never really felt as though she belonged in Beacon Hill, anyway. While she'd been gone, she'd considered selling the house and getting on with her life, but she just hadn't been able to.

Now she was glad she'd held on to it. With three children on the way, she couldn't very well expect to raise them in her mom's small, two-bedroom brownstone in Cambridge, no matter how comfortable she'd been there.

No, Peter's children needed to grow up in the house he'd loved, where she would prepare a nursery filled with three of everything.

It would cost a small fortune, but his trust fund had left her without any financial worries. She'd be able to raise the children and provide them with all the little extras without having to get a job and leaving them in the care of a nanny.

A couple of raindrops splattered on the windshield, and again she glanced up at the darkening sky. Although she'd wanted to get indoors and settled before the rain hit, she'd taken time to stop by the market after she left the clinic. She'd decided to pick up a few necessities, saving the bulk of her shopping until after the storm.

Still, the dreary late-spring weather didn't bother her in the least. She planned to make the best of it by putting on a pot of soup and by getting some baking done.

As she drove down the quiet, tree-lined street, excitement buzzed from her head to her toes. She scanned the old homes in the historic Boston neighborhood. Near the cul-de-sac, next to her own brick, two-story house, she spotted a familiar figure standing in his front yard— her neighbor, Hector Garza.

At well over six feet tall and whipcord thin, the handsome, dark-haired corporate-law attorney was an imposing sight. He always had been.

She remembered the day he'd moved into the neighborhood. She'd come outside to cut a couple of blossoms from her rose garden and spotted her handsome new neighbor watering his lawn. She'd stopped dead in her tracks and nearly dropped the shears, but she'd regrouped and reminded herself that she was married and had no business giving another man a second look.

The ploy had worked, of course. She never would have done anything to hurt or disappoint Peter. Nor would she have done anything that would have been disrespectful. But that didn't mean that she hadn't cast an occasional glance Hector's way whenever she'd been sure that no one was looking.

And now, as he noticed the arrival of the moving van, he turned toward her car, and she quickly averted her gaze to avoid making eye contact.

Some old habits were hard to break, she supposed.

So as the moving van slowed in front of her house, and she waited for it to park, she took note of Hector's yard. The well-manicured lawn and the impressive brick structure in which he lived certainly looked nicer than she'd remembered. Hector, who'd bought his once–run-down house in a distress sale, had clearly put a lot of work into the place.

He'd been newly divorced when he moved into the neighborhood, and she wondered if he'd remarried, if a woman had helped him turn the house and yard into a showpiece.

Probably. Those tall, handsome and successful types usually were involved with someone. But it really didn't matter to her if he'd remarried or not. She didn't have any plans to get too friendly with her neighbors, particularly that one.

Shortly before Peter died, he'd had some kind of argument or disagreement with Hector. Samantha hadn't known the details; Peter had only said that Hector was a jerk and that they should avoid him.

Avoiding the neighbors hadn't been a problem for Samantha. She'd thought that a couple of them had a tendency to be stuffy, which was one reason she didn't expect to get too chummy with them now. But a couple of days after Peter's run-in with Hector, Samantha had been carrying several bags of groceries to the house, when one of the paper sacks slipped out of her hand. A bottle of expensive red wine had broken, and her produce had spilled all down the drive.

Hector had been watering his lawn. When he saw what happened, he came over and helped her clean up the mess. His thoughtfulness and kindness had surprised her. Apparently, whatever problem he had with Peter hadn't carried over to her.

She'd always been appreciative when people showed her a kindness, so she'd given Hector a plate of brownies as thanks. She hadn't told Peter about it, though. He probably wouldn't have understood what she'd done or why.

But the truth was, she'd realized that he might have considered her attempts to avoid contact with him as arrogance or conceit, which wasn't the case. And for some reason, she hadn't wanted him to think badly of her.

So now, when Hector spotted her arriving in the car and their gazes finally locked, both recognition and surprise dawned on his face, somehow making him appear even more handsome, more imposing than before. And an unexpected tingle shimmied down her spine.

He lifted his hand in a wave, acknowledging her, and she automatically smiled and wiggled her fingers back. An innocent, neighborly acknowledgement, that's all it was. After all, she wasn't like some of the others who lived on this street and bordered on being snobbish.

Just then, the little tingle of awareness she'd felt when their gazes met somehow became a wave of warmth, one that settled where she hadn't felt anything in a long time.

Had to be hormones, she decided.

A quick glance in the rearview mirror proved her cheeks to be bright red, and she immediately broke eye contact, eager to separate herself from Hector and her runaway musing. Then she clicked on the garage-door opener and parked inside.

Using the remote, she shut herself safely away from the curious eyes of her handsome neighbor.

"Well, I'll be damned," Hector Garza muttered when he spotted a stunning blonde behind the wheel of a white, late-model Jag. It didn't take long for him to realize it was Samantha Keating.

Over the years, he'd thought about her a lot, probably because he'd felt sorry for her. She was too young to be widowed. Yet even before she'd lost Peter, she'd had a smile most people might call wistful. Hector had thought it was more than that, something he considered hauntingly pensive.

Either way, she'd always intrigued him, and he wasn't exactly sure why, especially since he considered married women off-limits—under any circumstances. Still, it hadn't prevented him from simply wondering about her, both then and now.

On the outside, Samantha and her husband had seemed happy, but Hector, who'd gone through a painful and unexpected divorce, had always figured a lot of marriages weren't all that happy behind closed doors. Or maybe he just liked to think that Peter Keating, who'd been born with the proverbial silver spoon in his mouth, hadn't actually had the world by a string. But that was probably because the two of them had butted heads shortly after Hector moved into the neighborhood.

One morning, while he was taking the trash cans out to the curb for the garbage collectors to pick up, he'd met Peter doing the same thing. Hector couldn't help noting that the Keatings' waste had been neatly packed in color-coded recycling bins.

The men had introduced themselves, and when Hector asked what he did for a living, Peter mentioned that he was retired. Then he'd chuckled and added, "My grandfather worked hard, so I don't have to."

Hector, who'd pulled himself up by his bootstraps, hadn't found the comment the least bit funny.

From then on, he'd nodded politely at Peter whenever they passed on the street or spotted each other in the yard, but that was about it. Besides, Hector didn't have time to socialize, especially with a man who didn't value hard work.

Then, a few weeks later, Hector was retained in a

high-profile case involving a big corporation and a group of environmental activists. The tree huggers had been making false accusations and stirring up trouble for the businessmen. And, it turned out their financial backing came from Peter Keating.

The next time the men met at the curb, Hector couldn't help saying something to Peter about his over-zealous environmental stand.

Okay, to be honest, Hector was concerned about the environment, too. He did whatever he could, but he didn't obsess about it. Besides, he had great respect for the corporate officers who'd worked their butts off to become successful.

Peter had bristled, tossing out a barb of his own about greedy corporations and the barely passed-the-bar shysters who catered to them. From then on, Hector had taken his trash out the night before, just to make sure he avoided Peter.

He didn't have anything against Samantha—other than deciding that she had poor judgment when it came to men. For the record, he'd always found the tall, statuesque blonde attractive. And he remembered the day she'd dropped her groceries in the drive, breaking a bottle of cabernet sauvignon and ripping open a bag of oranges that rolled all the way to the street. He'd never been what you'd call gallant, but without hesitation he'd headed next door and helped her clean up the glass and pick up the stray oranges. And then he'd helped her carry the rest of her groceries into the house.

She'd had a nice lilt to her voice and a pretty smile.

And in appreciation, she'd sent him home with a plate of homemade brownies—the best he'd ever tasted.

If she hadn't been married, he might have asked her out right then and there. But she *was* married. And to a guy he didn't like, although he had to give Peter Keating credit for having damn good taste when it came to women.

So, needless to say, when Samantha glanced at him from the driver's seat of the Jag, smiled and gave him a fluttery little wave, it had set his heart strumming and his curiosity reeling.

Had she stopped to say hello or been the least bit warmer or friendlier, he might have crossed the lawn to her house, welcomed her back to the neighborhood and worked up to asking a few questions—for example, "How have you been? Are you seeing anyone?"

But she'd used the remote to open the garage and parked inside, shutting herself off from the world around her.

Too bad, he thought.

He couldn't help wondering if she was still as pretty and shapely as he remembered.

Looked like he'd have to wait to find out.

Two hours later, Hector drove through the pouring rain on his way back home, his windshield wipers swishing at high speed.

He'd had a meeting with a client who'd been hospitalized with a serious heart condition, a meeting he'd tried to postpone to no avail. The stress of discussing an upcoming multimillion-dollar litigation couldn't possibly be good for him, but the CEO had insisted, much to the dismay of his wife and doctors.

And much to Hector's dismay, too. He'd heard the weather report and hadn't wanted to be outdoors when the storm hit. But here he was—on the road and finally headed home.

The wind had really kicked up while he'd been inside the hospital, littering the city streets with leaves, twigs and other green debris.

According to the forecast, the storm was going to be a bad one, and several inches of rain were expected. So he would have preferred to stay inside today, to watch the Golf Channel on TV and to kick back where it was dry and warm. But thanks to Bradley Langston, he'd had no such luck. And the guy wanted another meeting on Monday morning.

As a crack of lightning flashed in the east, followed by a boom and shudder of thunder, a branch from a maple tree crashed to the sidewalk, a large portion of it jutting onto the asphalt.

Hector swerved around it and swore under his breath, frustrated about being forced to go out in the storm and having to cater to the whims of a client with the proverbial type A personality, a CEO who was also a control freak.

Hector could understand Langston's concern about false allegations of sexual harassment, but most people would have put off business concerns until after their discharge from the hospital. Langston hadn't been the least bit worried about adding to his stress levels. So Hector had obliged him, reiterating what he'd already told the CEO over the phone, that both he and the entire law firm were on top of the litigation, that neither Langston nor the other members of the board of directors had anything to worry about.

Of course, Hector wasn't entirely sure that things would be that cut-and-dried. The case might not get thrown out of court, as he'd implied to Langston and the other executives who'd gathered at the hospital upon the CEO's request. Hector figured it was more likely that they'd end up settling, unless Langston hadn't been completely forthcoming about the details and something unexpected came out during the deposition stage.

But right now, Hector was more concerned about getting off the city streets before they became any more hazardous than they already were.

When he turned onto Primrose Lane, it appeared as though the entire neighborhood was battened down and waiting out the late-spring storm.

The moving van was gone, too.

Earlier today, when Hector had set out for his meeting with Langston, he'd been surprised to see it lumber down Primrose Lane and park in front of the Keating house. After all, Samantha had packed her bags and disappeared the day after her husband's funeral, leaving the property vacant for ages.

Hector could understand why a grieving widow might want to escape the memories of all she'd lost. In fact, if Samantha had sold or leased out the place, he wouldn't have given it any thought at all. But as far as he knew, she'd never actually moved out completely.

Every Thursday evening, after Hector got home from

the office, he could see that the gardeners had come by and manicured the lawn and yard. And during the summer, the automatic sprinklers kicked on regularly around 4:00 a.m.

He was glad she hadn't let the place run down, but keeping up an empty house for the past five years seemed like an awful waste of money to him. But then again, he'd never truly understood people who had such an abundance of disposable income.

Peter Keating had been a trust-fund baby, so apparently there hadn't been any financial reason for his wife to put the place up for sale.

Still, Hector had been surprised to see her back.

He didn't see any lights on inside the house now.

Was she even home?

He made a quick scan of the other homes on the street, noting that all the windows were dark.

Had the power gone out in the neighborhood? He wouldn't be surprised if it had. With as much lightning and thunder as they'd had near the hospital, it was definitely possible that a transformer had been hit.

As Hector pulled into his driveway, he pressed the button on the remote to open the garage, only to find it not working. Okay, so the power *had* gone out.

He left the car outside and entered the house through the front door, leaving his wet umbrella and shoes in the entry. Then he proceeded to the kitchen and out to the service porch, where he'd built shelves along the walls to hold emergency supplies. He wasn't what you'd call a survivalist, but he did keep plenty of certain things on hand: a first-aid kit, bottled water, canned goods, candles and matches, flashlights and batteries.

He had enough food to last a couple of weeks, something his immigrant parents had encouraged him and his siblings to do.

Jorge and Carmen Garza had not only instilled a strong work ethic in their three children and a desire to succeed, they'd also stressed the importance of being prepared for the unexpected.

As Hector reached for a box of candles, he wondered how Samantha was faring with no electricity. If she was anything like Patrice, his ex-wife, she wouldn't be prepared for anything, not even a broken nail. It would be dark before long, and if the storm or the power outage had caught her off guard, she'd be in a real fix.

Oh, what the heck, he thought as he snatched a few things off the shelves to take to her. After putting the supplies into an empty cardboard box, he returned to the entry, slipped on his loafers, grabbed the umbrella and headed outdoors to brave the weather.

Along the way, the wind played havoc with his hair and the flaps of his jacket, but he pressed on, fighting the driving rain and doing his best to avoid the puddles.

As a rule, he wasn't what you'd call a neighborly type and probably wouldn't have gone to this effort for anyone else on the street, unless it had been old Mrs. Reynolds, the eighty-year-old widow who lived three doors down. But her grandson had moved in with her a few weeks ago, so he figured she was okay.

"Dammit," Hector muttered as he stepped into a puddle that reached up to the hem of his slacks. He sure hoped Samantha appreciated his efforts to ensure that she wasn't stuck in the dark tonight.

He turned onto the walkway that led to her stoop, and when he reached the entrance to her house, he knocked loudly, then rang the bell.

Before long, the front door swung open a few inches, and when their gazes met, Samantha's blue eyes grew wide and her lips parted.

"I thought you might need some candles. I saw the moving van earlier, but I figured you hadn't had time to unpack everything yet."

Her smile, in and of itself, lit up the entry. For an instant, it was almost as though the storm had passed them by. "Thank you for thinking of me. To be honest, I don't have any candles or a flashlight, and I was wondering what I would do if the electricity didn't come back on soon."

They stood there for a moment, him holding the box and her holding back the door. Then she seemed to realize that, in his kindness, he was still getting wet as the wind blew sheets of rain onto the stoop.

"What am I thinking?" she asked. "Would you like to come in where it's dry? Maybe have some hot cocoa? I managed to light the gas stove and just made it."

Why not? he thought. Besides, his curiosity was killing him. More than ever he wanted to know what had brought her back after all these years. "Sure. I never turn down chocolate."

As Samantha stepped aside and away from the door, he couldn't help noticing that she was wearing an oversize shirt, which didn't hide a pronounced baby bump.

She was *pregnant?* Well, that certainly answered one of the questions he'd had. She must have remarried. If not, then she was definitely involved with someone.

He suddenly wished he'd declined her offer to come inside but found himself following her through the house to the kitchen, where the warm scent of sugar and spice filled the air, as well as the aroma of what had to be her dinner cooking.

So where was the baby's father on this stormy afternoon? Why wasn't he here with her so she didn't have to rely on her neighbor for help?

Hector probably should have handed over the matches and candles right then and there, but he'd always had a sweet tooth. And his curiosity wouldn't let up.

"I was surprised to see you today," he said. "I'd thought that you would eventually sell the house."

"I'd always planned to return home, but time got away from me." She nodded toward the kitchen table. "Why don't you have a seat?"

He took a large candle out of the box, lit it and placed it in the middle of the table. Then he sat down. He watched as she opened the cupboard, reached to the second shelf and pulled out a couple of lime-green mugs.

His gaze lingered on her face, then lowered, taking in the curve of her silhouette. Somehow her being pregnant made her even more beautiful. He'd heard other men describe a similar attraction in casual conversation, but he was genuinely surprised to experience the feeling himself.

He wondered how far along she was. She was about

the same size as his sister, who was expecting her first baby in August. So he guessed Samantha to be at least six months pregnant.

His curiosity was probably going to be the death of him someday, but he couldn't help wondering about her situation, about where she'd been, why she'd finally returned.

Why the hell did he find her so intriguing—even more so now that she was back on Primrose Lane?

He filtered his questions down to one—as a starter— and tried to coax the information out of her indirectly. "It's nice to have you back in the neighborhood. I'd come to think that you were gone for good."

"After Peter's funeral, I went to stay with my mom in Cambridge for a few months. It gave me some time to heal, but the months turned into a year. And before I could move back to Boston, my mom was diagnosed with terminal cancer."

"I'm sorry."

Her lips tightened into a firm line, as though holding back emotion, and she nodded. "Thanks. Me, too."

"So you stayed to take care of her?"

"Yes. I wanted to be there for her. We'd been through a lot together, and we were especially close." She poured the cocoa from a pan on the stove into the cups and gave him one. "After she died, I decided I needed a little R and R and took an extended trip to Europe."

She'd obviously been through a rough five years, and he couldn't blame her for wanting to escape. To take a break from responsibility, maybe. But he kept that assumption to himself.

"Anyway," she said, "I'm home now and looking forward to the future."

He glanced at her distended belly and smiled. "I can see that you are." That damned curiosity, laced with a wee bit of disappointment, pressed him to ask, "So where did you meet your new husband? In Cambridge or in Europe?"

"Neither," she said.

He opened his mouth to quiz her further, then thought better of it and lifted the mug to his lips instead. As he took a drink of the sweet, creamy cocoa, he was glad he'd taken her up on having a cup. Still, he couldn't help wondering whom she'd hooked up with.

Or why it seemed to matter.

"I didn't remarry," she offered. "Did you?"

He shook his head to indicate he hadn't, since he'd suddenly found himself at a loss for words.

There were plenty of women who didn't feel the need to sign a piece of paper to make a relationship legal, although he wouldn't have thought Samantha would be one of them. But she must have her reasons.

Life was complicated sometimes, and he realized it really wasn't any of his business.

Yet he couldn't help asking, "So, are you living with someone?" Then, for good measure, he threw out a little chuckle and added, "I'd hate to have anyone find us together and be uneasy about it."

"You don't need to worry about that." She took a seat across from him. "I'm not involved with anyone."

Okay. But there'd definitely been a man in her life about six months ago. Obviously the relationship hadn't lasted, and he wondered why. She didn't seem to be the one-night-stand type. But then, what did he really know about Samantha Keating?

As she slid her index finger into the handle of the mug on the table in front of her, the cup spun forward, slipped from her hand and spilled, making a chocolaty mess all over the table.

"Oops." She blushed and clicked her tongue. "How clumsy was that?"

She pushed back her chair and went to the sink for a dishcloth. As she moved across the floor, he couldn't help but watch her.

From behind, she didn't appear to be pregnant at all, but she definitely had a basketball-size bulge in front.

"I guess you could say that I'm going to join the ranks of single mothers." She turned on the spigot, wet the cloth, then wrung it out. "And I'm looking forward to being a mom."

Then her pregnancy hadn't been an accident.

"The baby was planned?" he asked before he could filter the question.

She stopped her movements near the sink, then shut off the water, slowly turned around and faced him, the damp cloth dangling in her hand. She appeared to be a little perplexed. Or maybe annoyed. And he couldn't blame her if she was.

"I'm sorry," he said. "I didn't mean to pry." Okay, so that wasn't true. He'd felt compelled to fish for information, but he couldn't explain why. So he concocted an excuse for it instead. "My sister is due in August, so I've found myself intrigued by pregnant women."

She placed her free hand on top of her belly and smiled, once again illuminating the room. "I had in vitro fertilization done at the Armstrong Fertility Institute. So, yes, the pregnancy was planned."

Now it was Hector's turn to feel clumsy and off stride. She'd gone the sperm-donor route?

What a waste, he thought. She wouldn't even have a romantic evening to remember it all by. And that was a real shame.

"What's the matter?" she asked.

"Oh, nothing." He took another sip of cocoa, trying to sort through the news she'd dropped on him, trying to get a grip on his curiosity that hadn't lessened in the least.

Samantha Keating was back in town. She was also unattached and pregnant. He ought to guzzle down the rest of the hot cocoa—which was really delicious—then thank her for her hospitality and hightail it out of here. But for some crazy reason, he seemed to be all the more fascinated by her.

And he'd be damned if he knew why.

Chapter Two

Samantha cleaned up the mess on the table, then carried the dirty dishcloth back to the sink to rinse it off. She wasn't exactly sure why she'd not only welcomed Hector inside the house, but offered him hot cocoa.

She supposed it was because she'd appreciated his thoughtfulness. Yet in all honesty, she'd also been a little unnerved by the blackout, by the isolation of being home alone on such a dreary afternoon.

As she'd wandered through the silent, memory-laden rooms of the big old house, she'd felt unsettled, on edge. The knock at the door had surprised her, but she'd been glad to see a friendly face. Chatting with Hector had been a nice diversion, so she didn't mind his visit. But she wasn't about to fill him in on all the details of her situation, no matter how nice he'd been, no matter how many questions he asked.

His curiosity about her pregnancy had seemed a bit out of the ordinary, even though he'd explained his interest, and it made sense.

She wondered how his sister was faring, if she'd had any morning sickness, if she had plans to take any childbirth classes, if she had someone to coach her through labor and delivery.

Samantha had been nauseous the first few months, but she was feeling a lot better now. And while she'd like to take the classes, she didn't see any point in it. A natural delivery was just too risky. Dr. Demetrios was going to schedule her for a C-section.

As the storm continued to pound the windowpanes, Hector reached into the box he'd placed on the table and pulled out a handful of small candles. "It's getting pretty dark in here. What do you think about lighting a few more of these?"

"Good idea." Samantha went to the cupboard and reached for several saucers on which they could place the votives. Then she carried them back to the table.

Moments later, there were candles flickering throughout the downstairs rooms.

"Would you like me to build a fire in the hearth?" Hector asked. "That would give you more light, and it will keep you warm, too. I've got some wood that I keep stacked in a storage shed in my yard."

"It's a gas fireplace," she said, "so you don't need to go back out in the rain. But if you don't mind lighting it for me, I'd appreciate it. Peter used to take care of things like that."

As her neighbor pushed back his chair, she watched his body unfold and rise. He was a big man, and the kitchen, which had always been roomy, seemed to shrink with him in it.

He moved like a man who was sure of himself, and she wondered what it would be like to face off with him in the courtroom. Intimidating, she suspected. Yet she didn't feel the least bit uneasy about him now and couldn't help studying him while he wasn't looking.

Some might think he needed a haircut, but she didn't. Those dark curls, still damp from the rain, made him appear rugged and rebellious.

She stared after him longer than she should have, until something sizzled on the stove. The soup, she realized, as she hurried to turn down the burner, to check the tenderness of the vegetables and to clean up the mess.

When Hector returned from the family room, he cast her a heart-shifting, blood-strumming smile. "The fire's lit."

She never had been able to ignore a courtesy, and a thank-you didn't seem to be quite enough. The poor man was still pretty damp from bringing over the box of candles.

"I made chicken-noodle soup for dinner. There's more than enough for two. I can also make grilled-cheese sandwiches, if you'd like to eat with me."

She expected him to turn her down, but instead he brightened. "Actually, I worked through lunch today, so if you're sure you have enough, that would be great."

"Good. I'll have everything ready in a few minutes."

"Do you want me to set the table?" he asked.

"All right." She handed him two sheets of paper towels to use as napkins, and silverware, then pointed out where he could find the glasses. "I'm sorry, but I haven't had a chance to do any real grocery shopping yet, so my beverage selection is limited."

"No problem."

They settled on water for him and milk for her.

The rain continued to splatter hard against the windowpanes as the storm battered Boston, yet inside Samantha's house, the candles flickered on the tables, casting a romantic glow in the room.

"You know," Hector said, "Over the years I kept expecting to see a for sale or lease sign in front of your house."

"I would have had a hard time selling or letting someone else move in. Peter really liked this house."

"You didn't?"

"Oh, yes. It's just that…" She wouldn't go into all the details about why she'd never quite felt comfortable here, about how she was determined to get over all of that now and make this her home.

"It's just what?"

"Well, the house was so big and empty after Peter died, and I was never comfortable staying here by myself."

"Are you feeling better about living alone now?"

"Yes, I am." The extended trip to Europe had been good for her in a lot of ways—some much needed respite, fresh surroundings, a boost in her self-confidence.

"If you ever get scared or uneasy, give me a call. I'm pretty good at chasing off bogeymen."

She smiled. "Thanks for the offer. But I've got a security system, so I'll be okay."

"I'm sure you will be." He smiled, revealing boyish dimples. "Again, welcome back."

"Thanks. It's good to be home." She placed a hand on her bulging tummy, something that was fast becoming a habit.

"By the way, I have to give you credit for going after what you want. Deciding to have a baby on your own was a big step to make."

He didn't know the half of it. "I'd wanted children for a long time, even before Peter died. So the Armstrong Fertility Institute made it happen for me."

She realized that he might assume she'd had issues with infertility while she'd been married to Peter, and while she hadn't meant to give him that idea, maybe it was best if he thought so. She couldn't very well go into all the intimate details of her babies' conception with a man her husband hadn't particularly liked. Besides, the first to hear her good news ought to be Peter's parents.

"Do you know anything about the father?" Hector asked.

"Yes, actually I do." A lot more than Hector might guess, but there wasn't any reason to give him more of an answer than that.

She slid a sideways glance his way, saw him staring at his nearly empty bowl with his brow furrowed. She assumed that he was struggling with her decision to raise a child without the benefit of a man in the house. He might have admitted admiration, but she suspected there was a part of him that didn't approve.

Yet she felt drawn to him tonight, to his presence, his kindness, his...friendship?

Funny how the first neighbor she'd reconnected with after moving home would be the one who'd had an issue with Peter.

After a moment of silence stretched longer than expected, he seemed to let the subject of her pregnancy drop by saying, "This soup is delicious. I'm surprised you're able to cook after just moving in."

"I'm pretty good at whipping up a meal out of limited supplies." It had been a trick she'd learned while growing up poor and making dinner out of whatever slim pickings she could find—Spam, fruit cocktail, stale saltines. Besides, she enjoyed puttering around in the kitchen, which had suited her far more than being a socialite had.

"Do you like to cook?" he asked.

"I do now."

"You didn't before?"

"When Peter and I were first married, I was pretty insecure in the kitchen. But then I took a few classes and learned to cook some great dishes. Now I love trying new recipes and creating meals."

"I'm impressed that you went to the effort, and that it worked so well for you."

"Thanks, but it really wasn't a big deal." She'd just wanted to please Peter, to be a good wife and make him happy he'd married her.

Yet when she stole another glance at Hector, she could see the interest in his eyes, the questions that remained.

Or maybe he was just being polite and a good listener.

Rather than risk any more personal disclosures, she laughed them off. "You'd be surprised at what I can do."

Hector was surprised already, and not just because the soup was tasty and hit the spot.

He was amazed that he was inside the Keating house, that he and Samantha were eating dinner together and having this conversation. And even though she'd answered each of his questions so far, there was a lot more he wanted know, like: What other talents did she have? And why had she stayed away so long before coming back now?

Sure, she'd told him that her mother had been terminally ill, that she'd nursed her until she'd died. And she'd mentioned an "extended trip" to Europe. But five years was a long time, especially when she had to pay property taxes and upkeep on an empty house in an upscale neighborhood.

He figured she must have really loved Peter a lot and assumed that it had been too tough for her to stay here after he'd died.

Then again, maybe it was just that she'd finally quit grieving and had decided to start living. The pregnancy certainly suggested that she'd put the past behind her.

He continued to eat in silence, to relish the taste of his soup—a rich chicken broth, tender meat, noodles and fresh vegetables. As far as meals went, this was only simple fare—but just the kind of thing his mother whipped up on a rainy day. And it sure hit the spot.

The wind, which had been blowing steadily for the past hour or so, seemed to die down some. The rain was still coming down, though, but it wasn't beating against the windows like it had done earlier.

The lights flickered a time or two, then kicked back on.

"Hey, how about that?" she said. "We've got electricity again."

"Just like magic," he joked.

She smiled, an alluring glimmer in her eyes that suggested the magic wasn't limited to the wiring in the house. Or was he reading too much into her expression because he *wanted* to see some kind of spark there?

Damn. She was a beautiful woman, and the fact that he found her so attractive was a little unsettling. He tried to shake it all off, yet even when he stole a peek at her profile, at the growing baby bump, he couldn't think of a better description of what he felt. Samantha Keating was a stunning beauty and as sexy as hell— pregnant or not.

And now that the lights had come on and extinguished the romantic aura, he needed to clear his head of crazy thoughts. It was probably best if he thanked her for dinner and left.

"Well, I guess I'd better take advantage of the lull in the storm and head home." He got to his feet and picked up their empty bowls, stacking them, along with their spoons. Then he snatched their glasses and carried them to the sink. "Are you going to be okay? Do you need anything?"

"Thanks for asking. I've got your candles and matches in case the lights go out again, so I'll be fine."

Yeah, but she probably wasn't all that comfortable staying alone. She'd said so herself.

But that wasn't his problem, he reminded himself. He'd brought her candles, provided a little company.

He'd already gone above and beyond the call of neighborly duty.

Their mess was cleaned up in no time at all, and he made his way to the front door.

"Thanks again," she said.

"No problem." He tossed her a safe, neighborly smile and stepped outside. Once on the porch, he opened his umbrella, then headed home. As he neared his front yard, he couldn't help glancing over his shoulder for one last look at the Keating house.

Samantha stood at the living-room window, watching him go.

The moment her eyes caught his, his pulse kicked up a notch. But he didn't look away. And for a long, heart-tingling moment, neither did she. Had she felt something, too? The attraction, the…chemistry?

Before he could come to any kind of conclusion, she slowly turned away and closed the blinds.

The momentary connection in their gaze had left him unbalanced, and so had his reaction to it.

He'd never been attracted to pregnant women before. Why would he be? Yet for some crazy reason, he seemed to be attracted to this one.

Or maybe it wasn't attraction at all. Maybe he was just drawn to her because she was so vulnerable right now. And not just because of her obvious physical limitations. He'd sensed an emotional vulnerability in her, too.

With her mother gone, there was no one to look after her—certainly not the father of the baby, who'd probably sold his sperm to a clinic, pocketed the cash and never looked back.

For a guy who'd learned to put emotions aside, especially in the courtroom, he sure seemed to be wallowing in sympathy for his neighbor. And maybe that was a good thing, a sign that he wasn't as unfeeling as some women might think.

His ex-wife hadn't been the only one to point out his emotional distance, his tendency to be cold and remote. Roxanne, the woman he'd been dating up until last month, had made a similar comment right before they'd broken up.

"You're insensitive to anyone's needs but your own," she'd said.

At the time, Hector had wondered if she might have been right. Maybe his job had hardened him. But he'd come to the conclusion that there'd been another reason he hadn't been too concerned with Roxanne's needs. He had to admit there hadn't been much chemistry between them, no real connection. So it hadn't taken much to make their relationship fall apart, and after an argument—he couldn't even remember what it had been about—it had been time to let go and to move on.

So now, in one sense, he was relieved to know that his sensitive side had kicked in with Samantha. At least that meant he wasn't as cold and unfeeling as Roxanne or Patrice had claimed he was.

He started to look over his shoulder one more time, then caught himself. What in the hell was he doing? That blasted curiosity was going to be his downfall one of these days, especially when it came to Samantha. You'd think he was actually interested in going out with her or something.

Shaking off the mislabeled attraction, he picked up his pace and hurried home.

After the blackout, Samantha did her best to forget about Hector's kindness, although she couldn't quite get over the fact that he'd caught her gawking at him on his way home.

Her breath had caught when their eyes met, and her blood had zipped through her veins—and not just because she'd felt a momentary rush of attraction or sudden embarrassment, but because it had seemed as if he'd felt something, too.

Had he?

As she'd turned away from the fogging glass, she wondered if he'd struggled with the same urge she'd had, if he'd felt compelled to take one last look at her, too.

Then she'd scolded herself for having such a wild and crazy thought. How could a man like that be attracted to a pregnant woman?

He'd probably just felt her eyes on his back and looked over his shoulder. Or maybe he'd heard a sound, a branch falling or something.

Either way, she had no business thinking about any man in that way, let alone a handsome and successful attorney who would be considered an eligible bachelor by any woman with a pair of eyes and good sense.

Her only focus in the world right now should be in creating a home for the triplets. So with that in mind, she'd shut herself in for the night.

She'd read for a while, then went to bed, where she slept fairly well, considering she was alone in a house that seemed to have more than its fair share of creaks and groans. Placing an extra pillow over her head had helped some.

In the morning, she'd had fruit, yogurt and granola for breakfast, then spent the bulk of her day going though closets and boxing up Peter's clothes and belongings, as well as the other things she no longer needed or wanted. She'd stacked the boxes along the far wall of the garage before she'd filled them. She would have to make arrangements for the Salvation Army or another charity organization to pick them up next week.

But even though she'd been careful not to lift anything heavy, her efforts had caused a slight muscle twinge in her lower back.

It was nearly four when she slipped off to The Green Grocer to stock up on all the things she would need to run a household. And when she returned, her car was loaded down with groceries, paper goods and cleaning supplies.

As she slid out from behind the steering wheel, she decided that her back felt better, but it still nagged at her. So she again massaged the pesky muscle. Then she circled the car, opened the trunk and surveyed her many purchases, which had been packed lightly into bright yellow reusable canvas shopping totes with The Green Grocer logo.

Before she could reach inside for the first bag, Hector drove up and parked in his driveway. She waved, and he headed her way.

He was wearing gym shorts and a Harvard Law School T-shirt, which appeared to be damp from a work-out. She couldn't help noting that he was toned and buff. His hair was mussed in an appealing way, and she found it difficult not to stare at him. But she'd already been caught gawking at him once, so she wasn't about to let him see her doing it again.

"Here," he said as he approached. "Let me carry those for you."

She really ought to shoo him off, to tell him she could take in the groceries by herself, yet it was nice that he'd offered to help, and since her back was only feeling marginally better, she decided to take him up on it. "Thanks, Hector. I'd appreciate that."

"No problem." He made easy work of the chore, taking several totes at a time, and before she knew it, he'd brought them all into the kitchen and placed them on the table, as well as the countertop.

"You sure have a lot of those reusable shopping bags," he said.

She'd had to purchase more than she'd probably ever use again, just to restock her pantry and cupboards. "I've got a few I can spare, if you would like to have them."

"I guess it's better than using the plastic sacks they provide at the store. So, yes, I could probably use one or two."

"Don't you recycle?"

"I would, but I don't do a lot of shopping. I eat most of my meals out."

Did that translate into: I date a lot? Or did that mean he was so caught up with work at the office and meetings he had to attend that he didn't have the time or the inclination to prepare meals at home?

Either way, she supposed it wasn't any of her business.

As she reached into one of the two bags that contained her frozen food, Hector did, too, and their hands grazed each other. She jerked back, more from the sizzle of his touch than the surprise of it.

"Whoops," he said, tossing her a smile. "It looks like we were both thinking the same thing."

That the frozen food needed to be put away before it thawed?

Or that that they were fated to catch each other's eye repeatedly, and drawn to touch?

Hector took several packages of vegetables to the freezer and put them away.

Samantha peeked into yet another tote bag, pulled out a loaf of wheat bread and placed it in the pantry.

After Peter died and she'd gone to stay with her mom, she'd paid someone to go into the kitchen, to empty the cupboards and donate the canned food and the dry goods to a local soup kitchen. So the shelves had been bare for years. But just last week, when the cleaning crew had been here, she'd asked them to wash all the dishes and wipe down the entire kitchen prior to her arrival.

She found herself actually looking forward to filling the shelves. Maybe a growing urge to nest was a side effect of her pregnancy. It made sense.

While closing the pantry door, she stopped to rub the small of her back, which was still a little tender. She suspected her pregnancy and her growing girth made her think about every little ache or pain more than she otherwise might.

Still, in hindsight, she probably should have asked

the cleaning crew to pack up Peter's belongings and haul them all out to the garage, too. But she hadn't liked the idea of a stranger digging in her closets and drawers and sorting through all of the personal items.

Yet even though the house and furniture were familiar, she felt a little...uneasy about being back on Primrose Lane. So much had changed.

"What's the matter?" Hector asked.

She offered him an unaffected smile as she removed her hand from her back. "Nothing."

"Did you hurt yourself?" he asked.

"Not really. I was just shuffling a few boxes earlier and might have strained a muscle. It's actually feeling better now."

His expression grew concerned. "You shouldn't have moved things around in your condition."

No, she probably shouldn't have. "I'm sure it's nothing."

"Sit down," he told her. "I'll put away the rest of this stuff."

For some reason, she didn't object. Instead, she took a seat at the table and watched him put the groceries and cleaning supplies where they belonged, instructing him whenever he asked—and sometimes even when he didn't. She hated to admit it, but she'd always been a little fussy about her kitchen.

He pulled out a small container of cinnamon, as well as the nutmeg and sea salt, and headed for the pantry.

"No, not in there," she said. "I put the herbs and spices in the cupboard to the right of the stove. I like having them handy when I cook."

His movements slowed as he turned to face her, and his head tilted to the side. "You're not planning to cook tonight, are you?"

"I was. But I'll probably just fix a bowl of cereal—something light and easy." She really didn't need anyone to tell her she might have overdone things earlier today.

"I've got an idea." His eyes, a pretty golden brown shade, brightened, and he tossed her a crooked smile. "I'll take you out tonight. There's a new bistro down on the corner of Fourth and Highland that I've been meaning to try. And I hate eating alone."

So he *did* have a lot of dates. She meant to tell him no thanks, which was the wisest thing to do. Yet she was giving his invitation a lot more thought than she should have. Although that was probably because she couldn't remember the last time she'd actually gone out, been waited on and pampered since her return from Europe.

"Come on," he said. "You'd like something tastier than cereal tonight, wouldn't you?"

Actually, she would. But did she really want to have dinner with him again? At a restaurant?

She should have made an excuse, told him that she preferred having a bowl of the Raisin Bran she'd just bought, but for some strange reason—loneliness, boredom or something else altogether?—she agreed. "When do you want to go?"

"I just got back from the gym, so I'll need a shower. But it won't take me long. Fifteen minutes, maybe. Unless you need longer than that."

"Give me twenty, okay?"

"You've got it." He tossed her a boyish grin, and her heart tumbled in her chest.

Uh-oh. She needed to get a grip. He was just being friendly and extending a neighborly gesture.

Or was he?

The next thing she knew, she was heading for the closet to find an outfit to wear. Then she would jump in the shower and put on fresh makeup. She probably ought to shampoo her hair, but she'd said twenty minutes, and she hated to make him wait on her.

Besides, going out with Hector was no big deal, she told herself on the way upstairs. It was just two neighbors trying a new restaurant in town.

Yet she couldn't shake the feeling that this seemed to be a whole lot more than that.

For some crazy reason, it felt way too much like a date.

Chapter Three

Hector couldn't believe he'd asked his pregnant neighbor out to dinner, but at the time he'd made the offer, it had seemed like a natural thing to do.

His sister, Yolanda, had told him about The Old World Bistro, saying that she and her husband had really enjoyed it and recommending it highly. So he'd planned to check it out, anyway. It didn't seem to be the kind of place he'd want to dine alone, so he'd asked Samantha to come along.

Now, after showering, splashing on a dab of aftershave and slipping on a pair of black slacks, a white button-down shirt and a sports jacket, he was heading over to Samantha's house to pick her up.

The storm had finally passed by, leaving the lawns and grounds wet, but as he walked next door, he savored the earthy, after-the-rain scent that clung to the plants and shrubs.

When he reached her stoop, he rang the bell and waited for her to answer. She was an attractive woman, so he'd expected that she would look nice when she swung open the door. But he hadn't been prepared to come face-to-face with a beautiful, statuesque blonde who could put Katherine Heigl, his favorite *Grey's Anatomy* actress, to shame.

She'd pulled her hair up into a twist, revealing pearl studs in her ears. And she'd applied a light coat of mascara that emphasized the biggest, bluest eyes he'd ever seen. Expressive eyes that boasted a warmth he rarely saw in people these days.

The adolescent in him wanted to utter "Wow..." but the man in him bit his tongue.

Had a woman ever appealed to him more?

He couldn't help scanning the length of her, completely forgetting she was pregnant until he noticed how her classic black dress fit snugly over her baby bump. Yet he still found her as sexy as hell.

But he'd be damned if he'd ogle her any more than he probably already had.

"You're ready," he said, making light of it all.

Her lips, which bore a pretty shade of pink lipstick, parted, and she glanced at her bangle watch. "You said twenty minutes...?"

Yes, he had. But he'd never known a woman who could pull off getting dressed within the time allotted, especially when it appeared as though she'd been fussing in front of the bathroom mirror for hours.

"You look great," he said.

"Thanks." Her face lit up, as if she hadn't been complimented in ages and had taken it to heart. Then she reached for her purse, which had been sitting by the door on an entryway table, locked up the house and walked with him to his car.

The soles of their shoes—his Italian leather loafers and her sling-back heels—clicked upon the sidewalk and echoed in the evening air, which was clean and fragrant after the rain.

Her shoulder brushed his upper arm, setting off a rush of hormones in his blood, and he had the strangest compulsion to take her hand in his. He didn't, though, and the fact that he'd wanted to made him realize he might have made a big mistake by asking her out to dinner.

But there was no way to backpedal now, so he shook it off, determined to enjoy a casual, carefree evening with his neighbor—even if he wasn't feeling the least bit neighborly.

Once inside his car, he stole a glance at her, saw her profile as she glanced out the passenger window.

Damn, she looked good sitting across the console from him.

Nevertheless, he turned on the ignition, started the car and backed out of the driveway.

Ten minutes later, they arrived at the bistro. He parked at the curb, just two shops down from the entrance, and escorted her to the front door.

A hostess in her mid-thirties stood at a podium and welcomed them.

"Reservations for Garza," he told the woman.

"Yes, sir. Right this way." She reached for two faux-leather-covered menus and led them to a linen-draped, café-style table in back, where a violinist played softly. Votive candles and a single red rose in a bud vase added to a romantic ambience Hector hadn't expected.

He pulled out Samantha's chair, and before taking a seat, she scanned the white plastered walls, the dark wood trim and the various pieces of art that had been tastefully placed throughout the restaurant.

"What a nice place," she said. "I don't remember seeing it before."

"It opened up about six months ago." He sat across from her. "I was told the service was excellent and the food even better than that. So I've been meaning to try it."

"Who told you about it?"

"My sister and her husband found it one day while they were shopping, and they've been raving about it for weeks."

"Your sister?" she asked. "The pregnant one?"

He nodded. "Her name is Yolanda, and she's my only sister." He chuckled. "She's three years younger than I am, but you'd never know it. She's been mothering me for as long as I can remember."

Samantha smiled and leaned into the table, clearly engaged in the conversation. "Do you have any brothers?"

"One. His name is Diego."

"So your parents had three children?"

"Yes."

Her smile broadened, and her blue eyes glimmered in the candlelight. "That's a nice family size."

He shrugged. "I guess it is." He'd never thought about his family in terms of the number of siblings he had.

Was she thinking about having another child down the road, maybe giving her baby a brother or sister?

He couldn't blame her for wanting to create a family, but you'd think that she'd consider adding a husband for herself, and a father for the baby. Yet that didn't seem to be part of her game plan, and he wondered why.

Had she loved Peter too much to consider replacing him in her life?

That was hard to imagine. But then again, maybe that was because Hector hadn't really liked the guy. Either way, it wasn't any of his business.

Silence settled over them until the maitre d' arrived. "Can I start you out with a bottle of wine?" he asked.

"Not for me," Samantha said. "I'll stick with water."

Hector ordered a glass of merlot from his favorite California winery.

"Good choice, sir." The maitre d' motioned for one of the other waiters to bring water for the table, then left.

When they were alone, Samantha leaned forward again and said, "I'm curious about your sister."

"What about her?"

"How's she feeling? When is she due? Has she taken any childbirth classes?" She gave a little half shrug. "Just that sort of thing."

"Oh," he said. "I get it. Being pregnant means the two of you have a lot in common. And now that I think about it, I've noticed that expectant mothers tend to gravitate toward each other at every opportunity."

"What makes you say that?"

"I've been with Yolanda at a couple of social events recently, and she's drawn to any other pregnant woman within fifty feet of her."

Samantha chuckled. "I'd probably do that, too. I'm going through so many physical and emotional changes right now. It would sure be nice to have someone to share it all with."

But not a husband?

Why had she gone the sperm-donor route to get pregnant? A woman as beautiful as Samantha shouldn't have had any trouble finding a man willing to donate his sperm—especially the old-fashioned way.

Hector certainly would have been tempted.

"You know," he said, resting his forearm on the table, "this really isn't any of my business, but I'm surprised that you went to the Armstrong Fertility Institute."

"Why would that surprise you? They're one of the most reputable and successful fertility clinics around."

Fertility? He hadn't realized that she might not have been able to get pregnant without the help of doctors.

"So it wasn't a matter of not finding a suitable man to father your baby?"

"No." She lifted her glass of water and took a sip. "Actually, I haven't dated anyone since Peter died."

That struck him as odd, and he couldn't help saying so. "I would have thought that a woman as attractive as you would have eventually found another man and gotten married."

"Thank you." She lowered her glass and her gaze at the same time, and he wondered if his compliment had somehow surprised or embarrassed her. When she glanced up, she said, "Actually, I never gave dating much thought."

"Why not?"

Hector's latest question caught Samantha off guard, and she pondered her answer.

For one thing, she'd been grieving Peter's loss that first year. Then she'd been so caught up in her mother's illness, in her suffering, in the failed attempts to beat the cancer, that thoughts of romance had been the last thing on her mind.

Looking back, she had to admit that she'd never even considered replacing Peter in her life. At least, not right away.

But then again, she hadn't been looking for a husband when she'd first met him, either.

Her experience with marriage had been a dysfunctional relationship between her mother and stepdad, so she hadn't seen a relationship as a catch-all/end-all. But Peter began to court her, which had slowly worn down her reluctance and proven to her that some relationships could be healthy and happy.

"There aren't many men like Peter," she finally answered. He'd had a kind heart and a gentle touch. He'd also saved her from a life of poverty and shown her that not all men were physically and mentally abusive.

"You must have really loved him," Hector said.

"Yes, I did." Peter had been a wonderful human being, a good husband, and she would never forget all he'd done for her. Still, she supposed, if she met the right guy, she might be able to love someone again. But with the babies coming... Well, there wouldn't be any men in her life for a very long time. She couldn't imagine anyone willing to take on an instant family of triplets.

"Lucky guy," Hector said.

Touched by Hector's comment, yet doubting it, Samantha smiled. "I was the lucky one."

As she glanced across the table and caught Hector eyeing her with an expression she couldn't read, something stirred deep within her, something she couldn't quite understand. Something that made her question what she'd actually felt for Peter, which was silly. She'd loved him, of course. How could she not?

"So you're not interested in dating anyone?"

She placed a hand on the upper ledge of her pregnant belly. "Come on, Hector. Who'd be interested in me now? Before you know it, I'll be bigger than a house. Besides, I have a lot more on my mind than romance."

"Like what?"

"For one thing, I have a nursery to decorate." And since she'd need three of everything, it was going to take all of her organizational skills to get the kids' room ready for their homecoming.

A grin tugged at her lips as she thought about how much fun she was going to have getting ready for her babies.

The wine steward brought Hector's merlot, stayed long enough to ask if they needed anything else, then left them alone again.

"You're obviously happy to be pregnant," Hector said. "And that's great. I'm happy for you."

"You have no idea how thrilled I am to be expecting. Unlike you, I was an only child. My dad took off when

I was a preschooler, and for the first half of my life, it was just my mom and me. So I'm really looking forward to having a family of my own."

The pregnancy was also her way of thanking Peter, of saying goodbye to him without ever forgetting him. Of course, she'd never forget how he'd rescued her, how he'd offered her a life of luxury that she'd never even imagined, how he'd loved her in a way no one else ever had.

Having the babies would also mark a new beginning for her, but Hector didn't need to know all of that.

Besides, what would he say if he learned that the father of her babies was her late husband, a man he hadn't liked? A man who'd been dead for five years?

No one, especially Hector, would be able to understand her decision. She wasn't entirely sure she understood the complexities herself.

"Hey," a cheerful female voice called out. "What a surprise. Look who's here, honey."

Samantha turned to the woman, a petite Latina who appeared to be about six months' pregnant. The man with her was tall, lanky, and fair-haired. He, too, seemed bright-eyed and cheerful as they approached the table where Hector and Samantha sat.

"You said you really liked this restaurant, but I didn't expect to run into you here tonight." Hector rose to his feet and extended a hand to greet the man. "We were just talking about you."

The woman offered Samantha a friendly smile. "We've been telling Hector all about this place, so I'm glad he took our advice. I'm Yolanda, his sister. And this is my husband, Chad."

Samantha had already made that assumption, noting a family resemblance between the siblings, even if there was a definite difference in size. "It's nice to meet you, Yolanda. I was hoping we would. I just hadn't expected to meet you here tonight."

"Really?" Yolanda turned to Hector and smiled in a you've-been-holding-out-on-me way.

Obviously, she thought the two of them were an item, so Samantha decided to explain. "Hector said you were expecting, too. I thought it might be fun to compare notes sometime."

Yolanda, who hadn't yet noticed Samantha's pregnancy, since it was hidden behind the table, zeroed in on her baby bump now. As she did so, her eyes widened, and her lips parted, clearly unable to hold back her surprise. "Oh, my goodness. So you are." She glanced at Hector, then to Samantha and back at Hector again.

It was, Samantha supposed, an easy conclusion to jump to: that Hector and Samantha were dating; that he was the expectant father. But she thought it was best if he clarified things. In fact, he'd probably be fielding a lot of questions from his sister when she got him alone, which seemed fair. After all, he'd been quizzing Samantha all evening.

Yet he seemed oblivious to his sister's assumptions and did nothing to set her at ease.

"How about lunch someday?" Yolanda asked. "I'm free on Tuesdays and Thursdays."

Samantha hadn't expected such a quick response, but her calendar was clear. "Sure."

"If you give me your number, I'll call later in the week, and we can choose a day that works for both of us."

Samantha reached into her purse, pulled out a pen and the little notepad she carried, and scratched out her cell number. Then she tore out the small sheet and handed it to Hector's sister.

She wasn't sure if the two of them would actually get together. People often said things like that upon meeting, but then dropped the ball for one reason or another. Either way, whether they met for lunch or not, she'd be okay with it.

It's not as though she was desperate to find friends, although in a sense she needed to connect with someone. For the longest time, her life had revolved around Peter and his family, then her mom. So she'd lost a lot when her husband died and even more when her mother passed away.

Besides, with the babies coming, it wasn't a good time to be alone.

There was a support group for expectant mothers at the clinic that she'd considered joining. It was just that she felt a little uneasy in a crowd, especially when meeting people for the first time. And for that reason, a one-on-one lunch with Yolanda was far more appealing.

"Would you two like to join us?" Hector asked. "We can ask the waiter to give us a bigger table."

Yolanda brightened, but before she could speak, Chad responded. "Thanks for asking, Hector, but I planned a romantic dinner tonight."

"Oh, honey, that's so sweet." Yolanda turned to her husband and smiled. "But it might be fun to—"

Chad put his arm around his wife's shoulders and drew her close. "I didn't tell you yet, but the company's got me scheduled to work a lot of overtime for the next month or two. So this might be our last chance for a special evening. And with the baby coming…?"

Yolanda nodded, then placed a hand on her brother's shoulder. "In that case, we're going to have to pass on joining you tonight. Maybe, when Chad has more free time, we can make it a double date."

Samantha waited for Hector to correct his sister about the date comment, but he didn't.

Instead, Yolanda added, "So what do you think of the Old World Bistro? Isn't it great?"

"I like the setting and décor." Hector lifted his wine glass, tilting it just a tad. "The merlot is good, too, but the jury's still out on the food. We'll let you know after we eat."

"Just wait until you try the spinach salad," Yolanda said. "You're going to love it."

Chad gave Yolanda an affectionate squeeze. "We don't want to keep the hostess waiting, so we'll let you two get back to your menus." Then he ushered her back to the table they'd been given.

But as they walked away, Yolanda glanced over her shoulder, taking one last look at Samantha, her curiosity evident.

Samantha waited until Chad and Yolanda were clearly out of hearing range, then said, "Your sister thinks that I'm your date tonight."

A grin curled the corners of his mouth, setting off a pair of impish dimples and a glimmer in those pretty brown eyes. "I know."

Samantha placed a hand on her rounded belly. "And she thinks that you've been hiding a big secret."

Hector chuckled. "It's going to drive her crazy until she learns the details."

"You kept her in the dark on purpose?"

"Yolanda's a great sister, but I can't help giving her a hard time every once in a while."

Samantha didn't have a sister—or a brother, for that matter. So she didn't understand the dynamics at play in the Garza family.

Would her three children grow up to care about what was happening in each others' lives? To tease each other in a goodhearted way? She hoped so. It all seemed so normal, so loving.

She glanced across the restaurant at Yolanda and Chad's table and caught Hector's sister looking at her again. Then Samantha offered Hector a smile. "Whatever you're up to seems to be working. Her wheels are definitely turning."

"If you think she's wondering now, watch this." Hector reached across the table and took Samantha's hand in his.

The surprise of his touch, the heat of it, nearly knocked the wind right out of her. As his thumb caressed her skin, her heart soared.

She could have pulled her hand away, she supposed. In fact, she really should have. But she was so taken aback by the bold move, so caught up in it, that she sought his gaze instead. And while she'd expected to see those impish dimples, a glimmer of mischief in his eyes that reflected the whimsical game he was playing with his sister, something entirely different passed between them, something blood-stirring.

Something *real?* she wondered.

Too real to ponder, she decided. The handsome bachelor sitting across from her was playing a game, all right, but on her senses. And so was the romantic ambience—the candles, the red roses on the table.

She clicked her tongue and drew back her hand, trying her best to regroup. "You need to stop teasing her, Hector. Or you'll really have some explaining to do. In fact, your phone will probably be ringing off the hook before you can unlock your front door."

He smiled again, but the playful glimmer in his eyes had completely disappeared, and a shadow of something altogether different had taken its place.

Something serious, something heart-stirring. Something a woman in Samantha's delicate condition had no business toying around with.

Then whatever had simmered in his eyes and had sizzled in the air around them faded as quickly as it had settled over her, leaving her to wonder if she'd imagined it all.

What had started out as an opportunity to tease Yolanda earlier this evening had morphed into something else the moment Hector had touched Samantha's hand and looked into her eyes, and his playful plan had quickly fallen by the wayside.

He tried to blame it on the evening, on the romantic setting, but he feared there was more going on than that, which caused him to withdraw.

They finished their dinner without another touch, another heated gaze, but he'd been on edge for the rest of their time together.

After paying the bill, he orchestrated a brief stop at his sister's table to thank her for the restaurant suggestion and to say goodbye. Then he and Samantha headed back to Primrose Lane. As they drove, he turned on the radio and found his favorite station. He thought a little music would eliminate the need to make conversation. And, for the most part, it worked, until Joe Cocker began singing "You Are So Beautiful."

He parked in his driveway, still a bit off-balance and eager to end the evening and set his world to rights.

As he walked her home, the moon and stars were especially bright, and the scent of night-blooming jasmine laced the air. Apparently, in spite of his best intentions, a romantic mood was going to dog him all evening long.

"Thanks for dinner," she said. "It was nice getting out, and the food was great."

"I'm glad you enjoyed it."

"Your sister was right. The Old World Bistro is wonderful."

"Yes, it is." And far more romantic than Hector had expected.

For a moment, he had the strongest compulsion to touch her, to cup her cheek, to press a good-night kiss upon her lips.

But that would be utterly foolish.

And so would lollygagging at her front door until he lost his resolve to keep things neighborly—and completely platonic.

"I'll see you around," he said, making a decision to steer clear of her for a while.

She nodded. "Take care."

As he returned to his car so he could park it in the garage, he realized that Samantha had made a quick escape easy for him.

Apparently, she hadn't read anything into that momentary rush when he'd touched her hand—thank goodness for that. Whatever crazy romantic notions that might have crossed his mind had been put to rest.

He heard her door close behind him, and it took all he had not to turn, to look over his shoulder.

But he didn't want to give her any ideas. And he didn't want things to become any more awkward between them. They were, after all, neighbors and bound to run into each other more often than not.

He pulled the car into the garage, then let himself into the house. He'd no more than opened the door, stepped into the living room and reached for the light switch when his phone rang. He took his time answering, assuming it was his sister on the line. Yolanda had been trying to hook him up with someone—*anyone*—for the past six months.

When he answered, Yolanda skipped the formalities of a greeting and launched right into the reason for the call. "Okay, Hector. What gives? Who is Samantha? Where did you meet her? And better yet, who's the father of her baby?"

"Hang on a minute. I just walked in." If he hadn't actually struggled with some real-life attraction tonight, he would have considered her inquisition amusing. But as it was, he didn't find anything remotely funny about it now.

He slipped the house keys into his pocket, took a seat

in the easy chair and kicked off his shoes. "I was expecting your call."

"Don't give me a hard time. You can't blame me for wondering. I've been trying to talk you into settling down forever. But maybe I shouldn't have bothered. It looks like you might have already found someone."

"Slow down, sis. Samantha is my neighbor. And since she's a single mom, I thought she deserved a night out. We're just friends."

"She's not pregnant with your baby?"

"Nope. 'Fraid not."

He could hear the disappointment in her sigh, and he decided to set her straight. "If the woman I got involved with was expecting my baby, my family would definitely know about it."

"I guess you're right. But you can be so secretive at times."

"Relax. Samantha's a nice woman. But no, we're not involved."

"I'm actually sorry to hear that."

"I'm sure you are."

Recently, Hector's parents had joined his sister in pressuring him to remarry, to start a family and to enjoy the fruits of his labor. According to his brother, Diego, they were proud of him and his Horatio Alger success, but they were worried about him and his nonexistent social life.

He'd tried to explain to them that a woman and kids didn't fit into his life, which was why his first marriage didn't last.

"Samantha is a beautiful woman," Yolanda said. "Aren't you the least bit interested in her?"

A bit too much, he realized. "Come on, sis. She's pregnant."

"I guess that means you're not attracted to expectant mothers, and I can see why you wouldn't be. I was looking in the mirror one morning and realized I was as getting to be as wide as I am tall. I started to cry—I do a lot of that these days—but Chad was such a sweetheart. He told me he loved me and said that I was more appealing to him now than ever before. He seemed sincere, so I sure hope he meant it."

"He did mean it," Hector said. "I can't imagine how exciting it must be for him to know that a baby was created out of your love for each other. And looking at you, seeing that the baby is growing and getting ready for birth, has to be a real thrill for him."

"Thanks, Hector. I needed to hear that." She paused for a moment, as if taking it all in. "So I guess that means Samantha's pregnancy is a turnoff to you since it's not your baby."

It certainly should have been, but for some reason, it wasn't, and he had no idea why. But since he didn't understand it himself, he certainly couldn't explain it to someone else. So he decided to change the subject. "Hey, I've got a question for you."

"What's that?"

"Even though Samantha and I aren't dating, do you still plan to give her a call?"

"I told her I would. And she seems like a nice person. Do you have a problem with us having lunch together?"

"No, not at all. I think it would be nice if you did. Her mother died recently, so she's pretty much alone."

"What about the baby's father?" she asked.

"He's out of the picture—*completely*."

"And so you're looking out for her?"

"I guess you could say that."

"Hmm. Now, that's really interesting, Hector."

He blew out a sigh. "Stop trying to read things into this."

"Okay, I won't. But don't you wish you had someone in your life again? Someone to come home to?"

"Not if she's like Patrice."

"You see similarities between Samantha and your ex-wife?"

Actually? Not a single one. But if he gave his sister any idea that he was interested in Samantha—well, he wasn't; he couldn't be. So he couldn't let Yolanda jump on an idea like that, or he'd never hear the end of it. And neither would Samantha, if the two women did end up having lunch together.

"So you're glad to be footloose and single?" his sister asked.

"Of course." He scanned his living room, which was cluttered with this morning's newspaper, a copy of *Golf Digest,* an empty beer bottle he'd forgotten to take to the kitchen a couple of days ago, a golf scorecard he was rather proud of.

If Patrice were here, she'd be bitching about how messy he was. Not that he didn't like a clean house; he wasn't a slob. If he spilled something, he mopped it up. And he never let the trash pile up until things smelled rotten.

He just didn't always pick up after himself. But he had a maid come in once a week, and she did the things he didn't have the time or the inclination to do.

And she never complained.

"You don't miss having a wife?" Yolanda asked.

"Why would I? I take my dirty clothes to the laundry, and my shirts come back starched the way I like them. I eat at my favorite restaurants, and for the most part, my house is clean. It's easier that way."

"But you're also missing out on love and companionship."

"I'm happy," he told his sister. "You've never heard me complain."

But he had to admit, at least to himself, that it wasn't all that fun coming home to a dark, empty house.

Or sleeping alone in a king-size bed.

Odd, he thought. Before Samantha moved back home, he hadn't given either much thought.

Chapter Four

The next morning, as Hector walked out to get the morning newspaper, he noticed quite a few of the neighbors had taken their recycling bins and their rubbish to the curb, which was a reminder that it was trash day.

Samantha hadn't yet taken out hers, either. And the truck always came early.

Maybe she'd overslept. Or maybe she'd completely forgotten it was Thursday.

Hector hated to think of her struggling with the bins and cans, especially in her condition. So even though he'd made up his mind to put a little distance between them from now on, he would offer to take her garbage out to the street for her.

He carried the newspaper with him, strode to her stoop and rang the bell. When the door swung open, he braced himself to see her wearing a robe, her hair tousled from sleep. But she was dressed for the day in a pair of black slacks and a light green blouse. Her hair was pulled back in a ponytail, which made her look a bit younger than she had last night. A bit more vulnerable—and sad.

"Did you forget what day it is?" he asked.

Her brow furrowed. "No, I haven't forgotten. But how did you know?"

"Because everyone else has already carried their garbage to the curb. I was just about to drag mine out and thought I'd offer to take yours, too."

"Oh," she said, her voice a gentle wisp. "You mean, it's *trash* day."

"What did you think I was talking about?"

"It's…" She tucked a loose strand of hair behind her ear. "Well, today was my mom's birthday."

Oh, crap. No wonder she seemed so down. "I'm sorry, Samantha. I guess this is going to be a tough day for you."

"I don't want it to be, so I'm going to drive out to the cemetery for a while this morning." She gave a little shrug and went on to explain. "It seems like the right thing to do. Then I'm going to go shopping. I'd like to buy some wallpaper for the nursery, which will give me something else to think about for the rest of the day."

In spite of his resolve to distance himself, he just couldn't do it. Not today. Not when she would be thinking about her mother and realizing how alone she was. But her plan to focus on the baby, on the future, was a good one. In fact, he suspected that had been her reason for getting pregnant in the first place. She probably wanted to re-create a family for herself.

"My sister chose a jungle theme for her nursery," he said, wanting to keep her mind on the baby instead of her mom. "You ought to see it. She and Chad had a lot of fun setting up everything."

Great, he thought. He'd just tossed out a reminder that she didn't have a husband, either.

"I'll bet it's really cute. I'm not sure what kind of theme I'd like. I've still got a lot of time to decide."

He couldn't help glancing at her belly, noting the size of the mound. She seemed to be even bigger today than she had been last night, although that was probably only a result of the clothing she'd chosen to wear. But still, he doubted that she had as much time to prepare for the baby as she thought she did—probably only a couple of months or so.

"If I find some prints that I like, I'll probably bring them home and think about it. Maybe you can help me decide which one to use."

Picking out baby stuff was the last thing he wanted to do, but under the circumstances, how could he tell her no? "Sure, I'll do that. It sounds like fun."

Fun? How lame was that comment? Hector wasn't into shopping, unless it was at Home Depot. He could hang out there all day. But looking for wallpaper with baby ducks and chickens? It would be pure torture.

"You could go with me," she said, "if you want."

Shopping? No way. He could still remember the time Patrice had dragged him to the mall to look for living-room furniture. It had been a pain in the butt, and they'd had a big fight that had landed him on the sofa for two nights.

He forced a smile. "I would, but it's a work day."

"Oh, yeah." She smiled wistfully. "I forgot."

Probably because her late husband was so wealthy he hadn't needed to work. It was a good reminder of the different lives they lived, the little they had in common.

"Just let me know when you're ready to show me some samples," he said. "I'll be home after five tonight."

She nodded and offered him a smile that made him feel like some kind of hero, when he felt like everything but.

So he nodded toward the road. "If you'll open your garage, I'll carry your trash to the curb."

"Thanks. I'll do that now."

Samantha went back into the house, and before long, the garage-door opener sounded. Moments later, she was showing him where she kept the recycle bins.

"The trash cans are on the side of the house," she said. "But there's just one, and it's only half-full."

He noticed a large number of boxes that had been lined along the east wall of the garage. Each was marked Salvation Army. "I see you're recycling clothes and things, too."

"Those were Peter's. I decided it was time to get rid of them. I'd like to see someone else get some use out of them."

The guy had always been impeccably dressed, so someone looking for secondhand clothing was going to get a heck of a bargain.

Still, he was happy to see she'd cleaned out the closets. That had to be a sign that she'd moved on.

Or maybe she was only trying to get over her husband and start anew. Maybe moving on was more of an effort than a reality.

He stole another glance at Samantha, saw her willowy shape, as well as a whisper of sadness in her eyes. Again he was struck by her beauty and the waiflike aura that seemed to envelop her, and something tugged at his heartstrings. She was expecting a baby and didn't have the support of either a husband or a mother, like Yolanda had.

So he would do whatever he could to make things easier for her, especially until the baby was born. At that point, her life would be full of wonder and awe, rather than grief and loneliness. Then he would back off.

"Well," he said, "I really ought to get moving. I've got a meeting first thing."

"Thanks for all your help, Hector. I really appreciate it."

"No problem." He carried her trash and recyclables to the curb, then returned home and got ready to head to the office.

Life was short and unpredictable, he supposed. People divorced, spouses died and loved ones struggled to carry on.

Maybe Yolanda had been right. Maybe he needed to find a nice woman and settle down. But he had no idea where to look—or when he'd find time to do so.

A car engine started up, and Samantha backed her Jag out of the garage and into the street. Then she hit the remote to lower the door.

As she spotted Hector, she waved, and he gave her a nod.

No doubt she was a nice woman. And if a man got involved with her, he'd certainly have to settle down. After all, he'd soon have a little one underfoot.

But taking on a ready-made family?

Hector wasn't up for the task, especially when it meant raising another man's baby.

Samantha had decided to get the visit to her mother out of the way early, since she'd be thinking about it all day if she didn't.

So after Hector came by and offered to take out her trash, she'd driven twenty-three miles to Hastings, where her mother had been born. Then she continued on to the little cemetery on the outskirts of town.

She parked and purchased a bouquet of pink roses from a vendor who sold flowers and pinwheels for people to place on grave sites. Then she made the short walk to the grassy knoll where her mother had been buried. Once she reached the familiar marble stone, with its carved cherubs, she took a seat on the lawn, which was still damp from the morning dew. There weren't many people out and about yet—just two women bearing a container of red carnations and a lone man in front of a double-size headstone, a baseball cap in his hands and his head bowed.

Birds chattered in the treetops, and a family of ducks swam in the nearby pond, reminding Samantha that life went on.

She sat in pensive solitude for a while, basking in the loving memories she had of her mother.

She remembered the day they'd spent at the seashore

when she was fourteen. The picnic lunch they'd eaten, their romp in the waves, the sandcastle they'd made. The chat they'd had about Samantha remaining a virgin until the right man came along, a man who would treat her with love and respect.

Several years later, while in her first year of college, she'd found that man in Peter Keating, a graduate student. He'd fallen for her quickly—and hard. With time and patience, he'd eventually convinced her that they were meant to be together.

Peter had adored her in a way most women only dreamed about, and at times she'd felt guilty for not quite loving him as much as he deserved. She'd talked about it to her mother once, about feeling as though there was something missing.

But her mom insisted it would come with time. And she'd gone on to ask, "Do you know how many women would give their left arms to be loved by a man like Peter Keating?"

Her mom had been right; it had come with time. Not the spark, but contentment and the realization that she'd done the right thing by marrying him.

She thought about her wedding day, when Mama had sat in the front row at the church, wearing a blue designer dress Peter had purchased for her. She'd looked every bit as elegant as the Keatings and their wealthy, high-society friends.

"This is the happiest day of my life," her mom had said, her glimmering eyes the same shade as her dress. "You have no idea how relieved I am to know you'll never want for anything."

And she hadn't. Peter had made sure that her life was picture-book perfect. And thanks to her quick thinking at his bedside five years ago, he'd even provided her with a family.

"Just think," Samantha said softly, hoping her words would somehow reach her mom's ears. "In less than five months I'm going to be a mother myself."

Or sooner than that, she realized, as she recalled what Dr. Demetrios had said about triplets coming early.

A monarch butterfly fluttered by, as if carrying her mother's happy response, and eventually landed on a dandelion nearby.

"I wish you could be here to see the babies when they come," Samantha said. "We would have had so much fun fixing up the nursery, shopping for baby clothes and waiting for their arrival."

She had Peter's mother, though. But somehow she couldn't imagine Marian Keating in a grandmother role, rocking the babies or changing their diapers. She'd be more apt to offer to pay for a nanny—one she interviewed herself and hired based upon credentials and references.

However, Samantha was going to be a hands-on mother, like hers had been. Of course, she was going to need help with the triplets at first. To be honest, she was a little apprehensive about bringing home not just *one* but *three* newborns.

"Don't worry," she whispered, her voice coming out a little louder than before, a little more confident. "I'll read everything I can get my hands on about childcare and parenting. And I'll hire help until I'm comfortable doing it all on my own."

For some reason, Hector came to mind. He'd been so helpful the past couple of days, and she'd been so lonely. He'd stepped in when she'd needed a friend the most, and she found herself thinking about him more often than not.

"I met a man," she whispered. "He's been really sweet."

She thought about Hector's intense brown eyes, his square-cut jaw, his broad shoulders...

On more than one occasion, she'd imagined that she'd felt a spark—or at least the hint of one. The kind of spark she'd waited for with Peter, one that, if she was being totally honest, had never quite materialized.

"Actually," she added, trying to put everything into perspective in an imaginary chat with her mother, "Hector is my neighbor."

But the trouble was, Samantha could easily imagine him being more than a neighbor, more than a friend. But she didn't dare voice that thought out loud.

Not even if her mom had actually been sitting beside her.

While perusing wallpaper samples in stacks of books at several different decorating stores, Samantha found quite a few that she liked. She narrowed it down to four, any of which would be darling. But one struck her as perfect. It was a farmyard print, with green and yellow tractors, red barns with silos, and the cutest little chickens and ducks she'd ever seen. She would have placed an order immediately, if she hadn't promised to let Hector help her make the final choice.

He'd been so nice to her the past couple of days, and

he'd said that looking at wallpaper would be fun. So, after the kindnesses he'd shown her, how could she not include him in making the final selection?

So she asked to take several samples, as well as a combination of paint chips, home with her so she could show them to him. Then she set an appointment to have someone from the store come and measure the bedroom walls next Tuesday. She was really looking forward to decorating the nursery.

By the time she stopped for a late lunch at the 1950's–style Coach House Diner and finished running the rest of her errands, it was nearly four-thirty. So she didn't get home until a quarter after five.

She parked her Jag in the garage, then carried her shopping bags into the house and put away her purchases. She couldn't wait to spread out the wallpaper and paint samples on the kitchen table. She still preferred the farm pattern, but she'd wait to hear what Hector had to say.

If she had his phone number, she would have given him a call to see if he was home yet. As it was, she walked next door and rang the bell.

When he answered, her breath caught. But not because she'd been surprised to see him home. She just hadn't expected to see him so laid back.

He was barefoot and wearing a pair of cargo shorts but no shirt. And while she tried her best to focus on those whiskey-brown eyes, she couldn't keep her eyes off his broad chest and well-defined abs.

Had he forgotten they were going to look over wallpaper when he got home?

"Hey," he said. "What's up?"

Okay, so he had forgotten. Now what?

As her gaze began to sweep over his chest again, she forced herself to gaze back at his eyes and to remember why she was here. "I brought home some wallpaper samples for you to see, if you still want to."

"Sure." He raked a hand through his hair. "Now?"

"Unless this is a bad time. If it is, it can certainly wait."

"No, that's okay. This is as good a time as any. Do I need to put on a shirt?"

Yes. No. Probably.

She again scanned the length of his chest, from the dark patch of hair that started at his throat and trailed down to the drooping waistband of his shorts and back up again. "Whatever you're comfortable doing."

"By the end of the day, I'm so tired of being confined in a shirt and tie, that I usually start shedding my clothes the moment I step foot in the house." He chuckled. "And after the day I had, you're lucky I'm wearing anything at all."

She was? She didn't feel so lucky. She felt a little… unbalanced by the sight of him.

And intrigued by it.

Impressed, even. His skin was an olive shade, without any tan marks. And he clearly worked out regularly.

He was an arousing sight, a picture of male health and vitality that any woman could appreciate.

She felt the heat course through her veins once again, pooling in her core, in the place that had been long neglected.

What was she going to do about her growing attraction? She certainly wouldn't pop over to his house unexpectedly after five in the evening on a work night ever again. God only knew what state of dress or undress she might find him in.

She managed to offer him a smile, hoping it didn't reveal her thoughts or her interest in him.

"Come on in," he said. "It won't take me long to grab a shirt. And then we can head over to your place and see what you've got."

As she stepped into the foyer, she couldn't help but scan the interior of his well-decorated house: the beige walls, the forest-green accents, the brown shutters, dark wood furniture and travertine flooring.

He had a gym bag near the door. A set of golf clubs, too.

She'd no more than entered the living room before he returned, wearing a white T-shirt bearing a Harvard Law School logo.

"See?" he said. "That didn't take long."

He walked with her back to the foyer, and as she stepped outside, he closed the door behind them. Then he followed her home.

"Thanks for taking a look," she said as she led him through her house and into the kitchen, where she'd laid out the samples. If she'd thought his presence had filled the room before, she hadn't seen anything yet.

He studied the bunny print, then moved on to the fairies and the rest.

"I didn't ask if you were having a girl or a boy," he said, "but from the looks of these, I guess it's a girl."

"Actually," she said, skating over the fact that there

were three babies and at least one was a boy, "I'd like to keep it generic. And for the record, all baby stuff tends to be sweet and might even seem girly."

"Okay, then." He pointed at the farm pattern. "This one is too boyish. I think you should go with the rabbits."

She looked at the bunny print, then cocked her head to the side. "What's wrong with the farm pattern? Look at those little ducks and chicks. They're darling."

"It has tractors, which isn't generic. It's definitely a boy print."

She crossed her arms, noticing how they rested across the ledge of her tummy these days. "I hope you're not one of those guys who thinks that little boys always have to be dressed in blue and can't ever carry a doll. Or that girls can't play with blocks or trucks."

"My kids can play with whatever catches their fancy," he said, "as long as it isn't dangerous."

"Your son will get to play with dolls?"

He seemed to ponder that for a moment, then said, "Sure, if he wants to. But I might encourage him to trade them for a teddy bear or stuffed dinosaur instead."

"Playing with dolls can help a boy learn to be nurturing and gentle," she said.

"Maybe so. But most kids learn how to behave by watching their parents. And when mommy and daddy show kindness and love toward themselves and others, the kids are more apt to follow suit."

He had a point, she supposed. Modeling the kinds of behavior and attitudes she wanted her children to have would certainly help. After all, it must work that way, because she'd grown up to be a lot like her mother.

"So tell me," he said. "Did you play with trucks and cars when you were a little girl?"

"Actually, I played with whatever I could get my hands on—plastic containers my mom kept in cupboards, an old box she brought home from work and I colored to look like a castle. Money was pretty scarce when I was a child. So I learned to be content with what I had."

His expression shifted from playful to serious. "I just assumed you were a trust-fund baby, like Peter."

She was now, she supposed, thanks to Peter's will. But it wasn't always that way. "Actually, I had partial scholarships to college and worked at the bookstore all four years."

"No kidding?"

"I wouldn't joke about something like that."

He studied her, it seemed. As if he'd suddenly seen something he hadn't expected to see.

"Does that disappoint you?" she asked, wondering if he'd somehow found her lacking, too. She'd always felt like one of the commoners around her in-laws.

"Why would it?"

Because there were others who'd thought that she hadn't fit into Peter's world. But she let that go unsaid and gave a little shrug instead.

"To be honest," he said, "I'm actually relieved that you're more down-to-earth than I thought."

"Why's that?"

He hesitated. "I wasn't all that fond of your late husband. And I'm glad to see how different the two of you were. It will make being neighbors a whole lot more pleasant."

She pulled out a chair, indicated that he should sit there, then took a seat next to him. "Tell me something, Hector. What did you and Peter bump heads over?"

He paused for a moment, as if needing to think over his answer, then said, "Behaviors and attitudes. I suspect our parents modeled two different world views in us, two different sets of values."

"And you argued?"

"Not exactly. Comments were made. Offense was taken. Bottom line? I guess you could say we just didn't respect each other and decided to leave well enough alone."

That surprised her. Peter had always treated people with respect. And other than Hector, she didn't know anyone who disliked him.

Deciding to drop references to her late husband, she turned back to the wallpaper.

"So you *really* like the bunnies?"

"Don't you?"

"Of course. I wouldn't have brought it home for you to look at if I didn't." She offered him a smile.

"Does it matter what I think?"

For some reason, it did. And not just when it came to the nursery.

What would Hector say when she told him there were three babies growing in her womb? And that each of them was carrying half of Peter's DNA?

And why in the world should it even matter?

After a little more small talk about ducks and chickens, fairies and unicorns, Hector got up to leave.

She almost invited him to stay for dinner, but she

didn't want him to think that she was trying to monopolize his time.

"Thanks for your giving me your opinion," she said.

"Anytime. If there's anything that's a given about me, it's that you can count on me to have an opinion."

She smiled as she walked him to the door.

"For what it's worth," he said, as he reached for the brass knob, "I actually liked the farm print best."

"But you said it was boyish."

"I figured you for bunnies, so I told you what I thought you wanted to hear."

"Why's that?"

He studied her a moment, as though trying to decide whether to level with her or not, then he winked. "Because you have the prettiest smile I've ever seen."

She couldn't tell if he was teasing or serious or both. And when he reached for the doorknob to let himself out, she was more intrigued by him than ever.

Chapter Five

After their little talk last night, Samantha decided that she really ought to avoid Hector, especially since she was finding herself more drawn to him, more intrigued by what he had to say. More attracted, she realized. How crazy was that?

After all, he couldn't possibly be interested in dating a woman with a ready-made family, especially when one plus one equaled five. So after a long, restless night that had her dreaming about all kinds of scenarios—including three darling little babies and a tall, dark and handsome daddy—she decided to keep to herself from now on.

And she would have done just that, if Hector hadn't rung her doorbell again early the next morning.

She'd been up for hours, or so it seemed, yet she hadn't expected anyone to stop by. When she'd swung open the door, her breath had caught when she'd spotted him standing on the stoop in a pair of khaki slacks and a pale blue golf shirt. She remembered that he had always packed his golf bag into the back of his trunk every Saturday morning before taking off for the bulk of the day. And that she'd seen his clubs in his foyer yesterday.

So why had he stopped by her house before heading to the country club?

"I'm on my way to the grocery store to pick up a few cleaning supplies and wondered if you needed anything."

"Do you always dress so nicely when you're scrubbing counters and mopping floors?" she asked.

He slipped her a crooked smile, and her heart slammed against her chest. "I have a woman who comes to work for me on Saturdays, and she told me last week that I was out of window spray and cleanser. But I forgot to pick it up, so I'm off to get it now, before she arrives."

Her gaze traveled the length of him, then back to those intoxicating brown eyes. "What time do you play today?"

His grin brightened. "In an hour. So it'll be a quick trip to the market. How'd you know that I was playing golf?"

"Just a lucky guess."

"So," he said, nodding toward his car, which was idling in the drive, "do you need anything while I'm at the market?"

"No, I'm okay. But thanks for asking."

"No problem."

As he headed to his vehicle, she turned to go back into the house, then thought of something she'd forgotten to pick up yesterday.

"Wait a minute," she said. "I'm going to empty out

the closet in the room that's going to be the nursery, and I've already run out of boxes. Would you mind asking if they have any to spare?"

"Will do."

He took off, and she went back inside. When he returned with more boxes than she needed, he asked if she wanted any help.

"No, thanks," she said, even though she hated to deal with the heavy boxes. "Go on and play golf. I'll be okay."

But she wasn't exactly okay. She was feeling way too many yearnings for her handsome neighbor. And she really needed to get her mind off Hector and back on nesting.

The next morning, when he spotted her sweeping the stoop, he crossed the lawn, took the broom away from her and finished the work himself.

If truth be told, she was glad that he had. It was getting harder and harder to do some of the simplest things.

But she had to stop relying on her neighbor to do them for her.

Three days later, when her doorbell rang, she didn't need to peer out the peephole to see who it was. Hector, it seemed, had taken her on as some kind of pro bono case.

And in the past week and a half, he'd taken her recycling bins to the curb on trash-collection days, which was especially surprising since he wasn't home very much and rarely had items that needed to be recycled—at least, not that she was aware of.

His kindness touched her, of course. And so did his boyish smile, the unruly hank of hair that flopped onto his forehead and the heart-spinning scent of his woodsy cologne. Just being near Hector had her thinking all kinds of wild and crazy things, some of them not the least bit neighborly.

She liked having him come around—maybe too much. What would happen if she got a little too used to his visits? What if…?

Well, there were a lot of things that could complicate her peaceful life, and she wasn't sure that she was in any position to deal with any more than what she was already up against. And for that reason, she needed to get him, her heart and her zinging hormones back under control.

So when she swung open the door and found a smiling Hector on her stoop again, she invited him into the living room, intending to have a little heart-to-heart.

"I was just thinking," he said. "This is a big house, and you probably shouldn't be doing anything strenuous."

"I'm not. The big stuff, like the moving, is over. And the Salvation Army will eventually come and take all those boxes in the garage."

"I'm talking about scrubbing and cleaning and vacuuming. After I saw you sweeping the stoop yesterday, I called Margo, the woman who works for me. She has a free day each week, so if you're interested, I can give you her number."

He was concerned about her doing too much? And he was offering his cleaning lady?

Samantha wondered if Peter would be that worried about her, if he'd been alive and known they were expecting triplets.

Probably, but Hector…

She pointed to the sofa. "Why don't you sit down for a minute."

He complied, folding his long, lean and masculine body into the seat and stretching his arm across the backrest. "What's the matter?"

"I really appreciate your thoughtfulness, Hector. But I guess it just seems…"

"Weird?"

"No. Not that. It's just…"

"Unusual?"

"Yes, that's what I'm getting at. I mean, you're just a neighbor. And, well, you didn't even like my husband."

"I wasn't fond of him, if that's what you mean. But I'm sorry that he died. Sorry that you lost him."

"Thanks. I'm sorry, too."

His sympathy surprised her, yet it seemed to make it all better. Or maybe it made it worse. She struggled with her reactions to him, both physical and emotional. But she'd be darned if she knew what to do with them, other than put a stop to their budding friendship—or *whatever* it was—before things took a complicated turn.

"I'm uneasy with your help, Hector."

"Why?"

"Because…" She didn't dare give her primary reason, so she reached for another. "It feels as though you've taken me on as some kind of charity project."

"That's not it."

"Then what is?"

"I have no idea. I guess you could say that I care for you. Maybe it's sympathy. Maybe it's a weird desire to look out for you. Hell, I don't know what it is. Maybe

I'm attracted to you." He laughed at that, and she didn't know what to make of it.

He had to be joking, but she didn't find anything funny about it, especially since her attraction to him was growing by leaps and bounds.

But she'd be darned if she knew what to do about it—other than accept his help.

And then where would that leave her?

The Armstrong Fertility Institute, a modern structure located near the Harvard Medical Center, housed the administrative offices, as well as a research lab and the clinic where Dr. Chance Demetrios practiced.

Since Samantha had been instructed to return the following week, she'd scheduled her appointment on Wednesday at ten o'clock in the morning. And she made sure that she arrived ten minutes early.

She was eager to learn that the babies were growing, that everything was just as it should be.

There were only three other women seated in the waiting room, and since there were other doctors who practiced at the clinic, it wouldn't be too long before she was called.

After the door shut quietly behind her, Samantha headed to the front desk so she could check in with Wilma Goodheart, the receptionist. Wilma, who was in her late fifties, had worked at the Institute almost since day one and seemed to know each patient by name.

As Samantha approached the desk, she said, "Good morning, Ms. Goodheart."

The receptionist, with her silver-streaked hair swept

into a no-nonsense bun, glanced up from her work and smiled warmly. "Hello, Mrs. Keating. You look bright and cheerful today. I take it you're feeling well."

"I am. Thank you."

Samantha had asked the woman to call her by her first name several months ago to no avail. Apparently, Wilma insisted upon referring to all the patients as either Ms. or Mrs., which was nice. But Samantha didn't like to be called Mrs. Keating. Every time someone addressed her that way, she felt compelled to turn around and see if Peter's mother was standing behind her.

"Go ahead and find a seat," Ms. Goodheart said. "I'll let the nurse know that you're here."

"Thank you."

Samantha chose a chair near the window and reached for a magazine. But as she did so, she couldn't help noting that two of the other pregnant women were seated next to men. It was nice to see expectant fathers be so supportive of their wives or girlfriends, and Samantha couldn't help being just a wee bit envious.

As she thumbed through the pages of the latest issue of *Parents,* her name was called. She looked up to see Sara Beth, the head nurse at the Institute, and smiled. Samantha had always liked the petite, red-haired nurse.

"How are you doing today?" Sara Beth asked as Samantha approached.

"I'm doing great, thanks."

Sara Beth, who held a medical chart in her hand, led Samantha to the scale and weighed her. Then she took her to exam room two, where she had her blood pressure and pulse rate checked.

"Everything looks good, Samantha. I'll let Dr. Demetrios know you're here."

"Thanks."

She didn't have to wait long, because a few minutes later, Dr. Demetrios entered the exam room.

He was a big man, with olive skin, dark hair and brown eyes. The first time she'd met him, she'd been surprised by how handsome he was. Based upon his professional reputation, she would have thought him to be a lot older, a lot more scholarly in his appearance.

"Good morning," he said with a smile. "How are you doing, Samantha?"

"Great. In fact, I've never felt better."

"I'm glad." He studied the open chart Sara Beth had left on the counter.

Since Dr. Demetrious was a renowned fertility specialist who divided his time between research and his medical practice, he didn't have as many patients as most obstetricians, so Samantha was glad to be able to count herself as one of them.

"Everything looks good," he said. "But we'll see what the sonogram shows us. I'd like to get a better view of Baby C."

After she got settled on the exam table, Dr. Demetrios turned his back to her and made some adjustments to the equipment, and she watched him work.

The last time she'd been at the clinic, she'd overheard two women in the waiting room whispering about him. From what she'd gathered, a former patient had once claimed that he'd impregnated her. The story made the gossip column and the society page of the *Boston Herald,* and Dr. Demetrios took a leave of absence to clear his name.

A DNA test proved that the child wasn't his, but the false accusation had shadowed his reputation, at least for a while.

Samantha wouldn't have held his personal life against him, since he was such a good doctor, but she was glad that the charges were unfounded. And from what she understood, he'd recently eloped not long ago.

According to the women who'd been gossiping, his new wife had been a waitress and a single mom. And Samantha had found the story heartwarming. It gave her hope that one day she, too, might find someone to love, in spite of being the mother of three children.

She hoped the doctor's troubles were finally over, and that his story had a Cinderella ending. After all he did for childless couples, he certainly deserved to be happy himself.

When the doctor had everything set up, he asked her to raise her blouse, then slathered her belly with gel so he could proceed with another ultrasound.

Samantha was mesmerized by the sight of her triplets.

"Baby C has turned around," the doctor said, "and it looks like…yes, it's a girl."

Samantha's heart soared with the news. She was going to have at least one of each, a boy and a girl. How cool was that?

"And Baby B?" she asked.

"Well, if it will move just a little… There we go. Another boy."

"Two boys and a girl," she said, smiling through the tears in her eyes. "I'm speechless. And so blessed. I don't know how to thank you."

Dr. Demetrious chuckled. "No need to do that. I just did my job. Nature did the rest."

She couldn't help giving God a whole lot of credit, too. And on the way out of the clinic and to the parking garage, she offered up a prayer of thanksgiving.

Then she climbed behind the wheel of her Jag. Before turning on the ignition, she stroked her growing belly. This pregnancy was the ultimate gift to Peter, to his parents. And she hoped they realized that.

They would be surprised when they heard the news—shocked, even. After all, it had been five years since Peter's death. But thanks to Dr. Demetrios and the Armstrong Fertility Institute, Samantha was pregnant with the children she and Peter were meant to have.

She did, however, suspect the Keatings would eventually embrace the news. Peter had been their only child and the love of their lives. Yet she still couldn't seem to pick up the phone and invite them over—or pop in on them, something she'd never done before.

Still, she'd have to tell them. And she'd have to tell Hector, too.

But for a woman who was bursting at the seams with excitement, she couldn't help wanting to keep her secret to herself for a little while longer.

On Sunday morning, Hector walked outside to get the *Boston Herald* and noticed that Samantha's sprinklers were on. He'd heard them go on at four that morning, but it was well after eight, and they hadn't shut off.

Water saturated her lawn and had streamed onto the sidewalk, over the curb and into the gutter.

Her newspaper, which had been neatly folded when the paperboy had tossed it onto the lawn, was soaking wet. Hadn't the guy noticed the sprinklers going?

Hector slowly shook his head. You'd think he'd be alert enough to put it on the porch or in the driveway.

Before retrieving his paper, he headed over to Samantha's house and knocked at her door.

She answered wearing a pair of jeans, a blousy top and a breezy smile. When he pointed out the flooding, her lips parted, and she stepped onto the stoop.

He noticed that she wasn't wearing shoes, which made the phrase "barefoot and pregnant" come to mind, and he couldn't help but smile.

"The sprinklers are supposed to be automatic," she said. "So why didn't they turn off?"

"There's probably a short in the timer. I can take a look at it, if you'd like me to."

"Yes, I would. Thanks."

As she led him through the house to get to the garage, he caught the whiff of something sweet baking in the oven, something that smelled awfully good.

Suddenly, the cereal he'd planned to eat later didn't sound very appealing anymore.

She opened the door, stepped down into the garage and pointed out the box on the wall that held the timer. "I really appreciate this. I'd call the landscaping company and have them check it out, but it's Sunday, so I'll have to wait until tomorrow."

"I don't mind." Hector took a look at the timer, shut off the sprinklers manually. Then he disconnected the apparatus for her.

"Thanks for doing this on your day off."

"No problem." He closed the little blue door on the timer box. "In the meantime, that doesn't do your newspaper any good. I'm afraid you won't be able to read it."

She crossed her arms and blew out a sigh of resignation. "How's that for luck? I'd wanted to check the weekly ads to see what baby things were going to be on sale this week."

"Hang on," he said. "I'll go and get mine for you to read."

"Are you finished with it?"

"Nope." He grinned. "I haven't even opened it. But if you'll invite me to taste whatever you're baking, I'd be happy to hand it over, along with all of the ads and coupons."

She laughed. "You've got a deal. And for the record, I made orange-cranberry muffins. They just came out of the oven."

"Sounds great."

"But I've cut out caffeine from my diet, so I don't have any coffee in my pantry. If you want some, you'll have to bring your own grounds. I have a pot and filters, though."

"Will do. I don't eat many meals at home, especially breakfast. But I try to keep coffee on hand for… visitors." He didn't mention that his houseguests were women who'd stayed the night. "Is there anything else I can bring back?"

"Not that I can think of."

He nodded, then went home.

True to his word, he returned with his newspaper and a small bag of Starbucks grounds he kept in the freezer.

Instead of knocking, he let himself in.

"Hector?" she called, when she heard the cricketlike chime indicating an open door. "I'm in here."

He followed the sound of her voice and found her in the kitchen, preparing a fruit platter of sliced melon, pineapple and bananas, sprinkled with blueberries. He couldn't help watching her work, watching her move.

But rather than continue to gape at her—and risk having her catch him doing so—he asked, "Is there anything I can do to help?"

She turned, leaned her back against the counter and offered him a heart-stopping smile. "No, I've got everything under control."

As her gaze sketched over him, and he sensed feminine interest on her part, which set off a flurry of hormones in his bloodstream. He didn't think he'd ever seen a more beautiful woman in his life.

If she weren't pregnant…

If she weren't Peter's widow…

Then what? he asked himself. Would he actually hit on her?

Yes, he realized. He would. Then why let anything stop him now?

When the answer failed to form, he shook off the

thought and handed her the coffee. Then he took a seat in the breakfast nook, at the table she'd already set.

A big bay window looked out into the backyard, which boasted a lawn big enough for a game of T-ball and a tree that would be perfect for climbing.

Samantha's son or daughter would be lucky to grow up in this house. And as Samantha served the fruit and muffins on a china plate, he realized the kid would be lucky to have her for a mom.

As the coffee began to dribble into the carafe, she joined him at the table, saying, "Feel free to read the paper while you eat."

As Hector took a bite of one of the best muffins he'd ever eaten, he sorted through the newspaper until he came across a department store advertisement that displayed baby things. Then he handed the page to Samantha. "Is this what you were looking for?"

She brightened as she took it from him. "Oh, how sweet. I really like that white crib. And it has a matching dresser and changing table." She set the section she'd been reading back on the table and pointed at the furniture that had caught her eye. "Isn't it cute?"

It looked like any old crib to him—white, with rails so the kid wouldn't fall out. He didn't see anything especially cute about it. He did, however, think Samantha was pretty damn cute herself, even if she was pregnant.

Hell, maybe even because of it.

He'd told her once that pregnant women intrigued him these days, which really wasn't true. She was the only one who had actually caught his interest.

But maybe he'd be wise not to stew about it.

"You know," he said, "you've got a lot of things you're going to need to buy before the baby gets here, unless someone's going to throw you a shower."

"Oh. No, I don't think so. I'm not sure who'd have one for me, but that's okay. I really won't need one."

He supposed she had enough money to purchase everything herself, but his sister and his mother really enjoyed going to showers—for both babies and brides. It seemed to be a big deal to them, and they would "ooh" and "ahh" over the gifts they'd bought. Then they'd make a big deal about getting dressed up for the event.

So Hector figured that Samantha would enjoy having one. But if she hadn't told people she was back, or if she hadn't maintained any friendships in Boston, he realized there might not be anyone to host it.

Too bad, he thought, feeling sorry for her yet again.

"Would you like another muffin?" she asked.

"Sure." While she stood to serve him, he couldn't help adding, "The baby's going to be here before you know it."

"I know, but there's still plenty of time."

Maybe only a couple of months, he guessed, which wasn't all that long. She really needed to look ahead, to prepare for the unexpected, especially since she didn't have anyone to help her.

"Don't some babies come early?" he asked, trying to send a subtle message.

"Yes, they do. And mine probably will." She returned with a plate of muffins, then sat down and reached for the advertisement. As she scanned the vast assortment of baby furniture, supplies and clothing, she didn't appear to be overly concerned, which he couldn't understand. Especially if she thought her baby might be one that came early.

He was just about to prod her a little more, when she said, "Maybe I better go shopping this week. With all I need to buy, I want to take advantage of the sale price."

Good. He'd made his point, so he settled back in his seat.

They continued to eat until the coffee stopped brewing with a tired wheeze.

"It's ready," Samantha said as she pushed back her chair and stood once again. Then she went to the cupboard and filled Hector's mug.

On her way back to the table, she caught him studying her, the swell of her belly. As his eyes lifted, their gazes met and locked. Something warm stirred between them, something that set off a zing in her pulse, and she couldn't help feeling a little…amazed by it all.

Trying to pretend it hadn't happened, she asked, "Do you use cream and sugar?"

"No, this is fine. Thanks." Hector took the mug in both hands, but didn't take a sip. "By the way, did you ever order that wallpaper?"

"Yes, I got the farm print that we both liked, but it's on back order. Hopefully, I'll have it within a week. I also chose the blue paint for the walls and the white for the crown molding."

"The baby ought to like that."

"I hope so."

After Hector had eaten his fill, he picked up the front page of the newspaper and scanned the headlines.

Samantha, too, sorted through the pages until she found the society section, something she'd read daily when she'd been married to Peter but hadn't given much thought to reading these days.

But why should she? She'd quit seeing all of her old friends when she married Peter, and she hadn't really been all that close to the women she'd met after they'd become a couple. Then, after he died, life just wasn't the same anymore.

Still, she studied the photos, wondering if she would recognize anyone she knew.

There were the usual wedding announcements, but her gaze was drawn to a picture that touched her heart— an adoption celebration that was held at the Boston Children's Home yesterday.

"What a sweet story," she said.

Hector looked up from his reading. "What's that?"

"There was a big celebration held at the Children's Home yesterday afternoon, and if I had known about it, I would have stopped by."

"What were they celebrating?"

"Do you know Olivia Mallory?"

"The name sounds familiar."

"She's the daughter of Dr. Gerald Armstrong, the man who founded the Armstrong Institute. And she's married to Jamison Mallory."

"The junior senator?"

"Yes. She's also the president of the board of directors of the Children's Home and has volunteered there for years."

"I take it that you know her personally. Is she a friend?"

"Yes, but I haven't seen her in a long time."

Samantha and Olivia had run in the same circle when Peter had been alive. And she was one of the few women in that crowd Samantha had actually felt comfortable around.

"Olivia and Jamison have adopted two orphaned brothers, a seven-year-old named Kevin, and Danny, who's three." She turned the paper so he could see the photo.

"Cute kids," Hector said.

"They're darling. And they actually resemble Olivia. If I didn't know they were adopted, I'd assume Olivia had given birth to them."

"Does Olivia know you're back in town?"

"I don't think so."

"Maybe you should call her."

It struck her as odd that he'd make that suggestion, but it was one she'd already considered. It would be nice to renew their friendship. "Later this morning, I'll give her a call to congratulate her." And maybe she'd ask if they could meet for lunch one day soon.

Samantha took one last look at the photo of Olivia and her sons before moving on to another article about a benefit that was held at the Belle Fleur Country Club. The proceeds of a silent auction would fund scholarships for underprivileged high-school seniors.

In one of several photos that accompanied that spread, she spotted her in-laws—front and center.

They looked great, she decided. And they seemed to be in good spirits.

She'd stayed in contact with Randall and Marian

Keating after Peter's death, calling about once a month and having dinner on birthdays. She wasn't hurt that they'd seemed to pull away over the years. She assumed that seeing her was painful for them.

Truth be told, she'd never felt fully connected to or accepted by them before, and since Peter was gone, their pulling away only served to make the chasm deeper.

She really hoped that the news of the babies would correct that, and again she wondered how they would feel when she told them.

Admittedly, she was really dragging her feet, although she wasn't sure why. At one time, she'd wanted nothing more than to be totally accepted by them, to be considered a Keating in every sense of the name.

Maybe, deep inside, she was afraid of how Marian was going to handle the news. She suspected that she'd be happy, but the woman had been so hard to please when Peter was alive.

There was a strong possibility that Peter's mother would try to tell Samantha how to raise the children, advice that wouldn't be welcome. But in the past five years, she'd come to believe she was more ready for a face-off, if one became necessary.

The newsprint crinkled as Hector set the front page of the business section on the table, drawing Samantha from her musing.

"It looks like the Armstrong Fertility Institute is experiencing some serious financial problems," he said.

"Oh, really?"

He nodded, his expression intense as he glanced back at the article he'd just read.

"What happened?"

"It's not clear, but it sounds to me as if it's more than just mishandling funds or some poor business decisions."

Samantha lowered the paper she'd been reading. "Are you suggesting that something criminal might be going on?"

He shrugged. "It's hard to say, but you can bet the media is going to keep a close eye on it."

"I hope that's not the case," Samantha said. "The Institute and the doctors there have been a real blessing to childless couples all over the country."

Hector glanced across the table at her and smiled. "I'm sure they've been a blessing to you."

Three times the blessing, she thought. But although she'd been tempted a couple of times, she still couldn't quite bring herself to tell Hector she was carrying triplets.

Or that Peter was their father.

Chapter Six

Samantha waited two hours on Tuesday for the painter to arrive and give her an estimate on the cost of painting the nursery. He called once to tell her he was running late.

When he finally showed up, the lanky fellow took off his paint-splattered cap, revealing a shock of red hair. "I'm really sorry for being late."

He'd said that before, and since she was a little annoyed, she didn't respond to his apology. Instead, she led him to the soon-to-be nursery.

"I pride myself on being prompt," he said, "and providing a professional service. I hope you don't think that this sort of thing happens very often."

"It's okay," she said, letting him off the hook. "I didn't have anything pressing to do this afternoon."

"Good, but that's not the point."

She led him down the hall, thinking he'd let the issue drop.

"My four-year-old son was running a fever," the man explained, "and his preschool called. My wife's out of town, which left things up to me. My mother usually steps in to help, but she was having some tests run at the medical center, so I had to pick him up and wait with him at home until she could relieve me. I'm afraid that threw off my schedule for the rest of the day."

"I understand," Samantha said, realizing that his excuse was a good one. And that if it had happened to her, she… Well, she would have chosen her child over an appointment, too. But unlike the painter and his son, she and her kids wouldn't have a grandma to step in to help when the unexpected happened.

Of course, they would have Marian Keating, but Peter's mother wasn't the warm, nurturing type. Peter had insisted that his mom had been different when he was a kid, but Samantha hadn't ever seen that side of her mother-in-law.

At times like this, when she was reminded of all she'd lost when her mother died, Samantha got a little sad. But she wasn't about to lose it and start sniffling in front of the painter, so she took a deep, calming breath.

"This is it," she said, pointing inside the room. "I'm going to have wallpaper on two of the walls and a border along the edge of the ceiling. I'll also need the inside of the closet painted."

"All right." He took some measurements, then reached for his clipboard and scratched out the estimate on a bid form. When he'd finished, he tore off the top copy and handed it to her.

She looked it over and decided the price was reasonable. "This works for me. How long will it take? And when can you start?"

"I can get it all done in a day. And I can start tomorrow, if you'd like. Work's been pretty slow lately. In fact, that's what my wife is doing out of town—interviewing for a job. It'll mean a heck of a commute for her, but…well, things have been a little tight."

And they had a son, she thought, a preschooler who was sick today.

Her heart, which seemed to be especially soft and sympathetic these days, went out to the man.

"You know," she said, "the rest of the house could use some paint, too."

He brightened. "If you'll let me do it, I'll give you a great deal."

She wasn't as concerned about the price as she was about providing the man with some work. "Why don't you give me an estimate for that, too?"

After he measured the rest of the house, he gave her a revised price. Normally, she would have gotten another bid on a project. That is, if the walls had really needed a fresh coat of paint, and they didn't. But the man and his family were struggling financially, and she was in a position to help.

She'd also been thinking about redecorating. She wanted to give the house a new look, to make it more child-friendly instead of having the Marian Keating stamp of approval. So she took the time to choose the colors she liked from some sample sheets he pulled from the clipboard and told the painter he could start tomorrow.

She followed him to the door, and as he stepped outside, Hector's car turned into his driveway. She waved at him, and as the painter climbed behind the wheel of his pickup and started the engine, Hector parked and headed toward her house.

She waited for him, noting how nice he looked in a tie, how professional. Yet he wore a crooked grin that suggested there was a boyish side that seemed to balance him out.

He nodded toward the departing pickup. "Is that the painter?"

"Yes. He's going to start tomorrow." She tucked a strand of hair behind her ear. "I decided to go ahead and have him paint the entire place."

Hector furrowed his brow. "Where are you going to go?"

"Go?"

"You can't sleep there. The fumes won't be good for you or the baby."

He was right, of course. And she would have come to that conclusion eventually. She'd only planned to paint the nursery, so she would have just closed the bedroom door to shut out the smell and opened the windows in the rest of the house.

But with all of the rooms being painted? She'd definitely have to move out for a couple of days.

"I guess I hadn't thought quite that far. I'll just have to go to a hotel."

Hector seemed to ponder her response, but only for

a moment. "I'll tell you what. Pack up some things and come stay with me until the house is finished. You can sleep in my guestroom."

"Oh, no. I can't do that."

"Why not?"

She couldn't come up with an immediate reason, at least not one she was willing to share with him. She wasn't about to say that moving in with him for a couple of days sounded way too appealing, and that the mere thought of it had sent her heartbeat hammering in her chest.

So she said, "Thanks for the offer, but I think staying at a hotel would be easier."

"Easier than walking twenty yards? Besides, if you forget anything, I can go into your house and get it for you."

"That's really thoughtful, Hector, but I don't want to put you out."

He laughed. "You're not putting me out. The way I see it, I'm taking full advantage of the situation."

What did he mean by that? Was he hoping to get her into bed?

"If I'm lucky," he added, "I just might get some more homemade muffins out of it."

Okay, so she'd taken a great big leap and missed his point altogether, which was the problem with staying in his guestroom. Her thoughts were getting way out of hand, and he was only trying to be neighborly.

He tossed her a smile that turned her heart end over end. "I could pick up a DVD on the way home from the office, and we could kick back and watch a movie. What do you say?"

It might be fun. And it would certainly be better than staying alone in a hotel room. Just the thought of packing her things made her weary, and staying in an impersonal room at a hotel wasn't very appealing.

Besides, what was she worried about? She'd been wrong about Hector. He was just being nice—for whatever reason. She was the one with the problem—the out-of-control hormones that had her imagination running amok.

"All right," she said, crossing her arms and resting them on her belly. "We can eat popcorn and think of it as a slumber party."

Hey, why not? A lot of women had friends who were male.

"I've never been invited to a slumber party," he said, "unless you count the one Bobby Garcia and I crashed."

"You crashed a girl's sleepover?"

"Yep. And we tapped on windows, rattled chains and made ghostly howls outside their family room. Needless to say, we scared the bejeezus out of them, and when they all started screaming, Cindy's mom called the police. Bobby and I ran like hell as soon as we heard the sirens."

Samantha laughed. "I used to know boys like you."

"What can I say? Some of us never really grow up." He tossed her a playful grin, and as he turned to walk away, he added, "I'll see you tomorrow morning."

She nodded, but as he headed home, her thoughts were on tonight and his plans for the evening. What was he going to do between now and morning? Already her house felt empty without him there.

But she didn't dare ask. If he had a date, she didn't want to hear about it. News like that might bother her in a way that it shouldn't.

Besides, he was probably right. Staying with him would be better than staying in a hotel, which would be awfully lonely.

And quite frankly, she'd had enough silence over the last few months to last her a lifetime.

She and Hector had developed a closeness these past few days she hadn't expected them to have. Of course, the male/female attraction thing on her part still boggled her mind, but the closer she got to her due date, and the bigger the triplets grew, the less she would think about romance.

Besides, she needed a friend. And as odd as it sounded, she seemed to have found one right next door—in Hector.

The next morning, before the painter arrived, Samantha packed an overnight bag to take to Hector's. She also rifled through the kitchen pantry, looking for all the ingredients she would need to fix dinner for the next couple of nights, including salt, pepper and spices.

By his own admission, he had a cupboard that rivaled Old Mother Hubbard's. So assuming he would have very few items to contribute to the evening meal, she loaded up a Green Grocer tote. Then she hauled it, as well as her overnight bag, to his house.

When he answered the door and found her on the stoop, he reached for the bags. "Let me take those." As he stepped aside, allowing her in, he peeked into the tote, which was stuffed full. "What's this?"

"I thought I'd cook dinner for you tonight, to say thanks for letting me stay."

"Ordinarily I'd protest, but I haven't had a home-cooked meal in ages. This is great." He led her through the living room, which was tastefully decorated in shades of green and brown. Dark wood cabinets and furniture, a chocolate-colored Italian leather sofa and glass-topped accent tables, definitely gave it a masculine flavor, yet it was also appealing to a woman.

Or maybe Samantha found it appealing because it reflected Hector's personality, his style.

When he showed her the kitchen, which was a lot roomier than her own, she noticed an expanse of green Corian countertops and shiny stainless-steel appliances. She knew it didn't get much use, so she was looking forward to breaking it in.

"What would you like for dinner?" she asked.

"Surprise me."

"All right. Do you have any food allergies? Any likes or dislikes?"

"I'm not big on onions, although I'll eat them as long as they're not raw."

"I'll keep that in mind."

"But don't feel as though you have to go out of your way for me," he said. "I can pick up something for us and bring it home."

"I enjoy cooking, remember?"

He tossed her a heart-spinning grin. "Then *mi casa es su casa*—my house is yours."

After he placed the grocery tote on the counter, he

helped her put away the things that needed to be refrig-
erated.

"What are you going to do with the ground turkey
meat?" he asked.

"I'm surprising you, remember?"

"Okay, but I probably should tell you that I'm not all
that keen on turkey."

"That's okay. You'll never know you're eating it."

He looked skeptical. "Promise?"

She lifted her hand in a Scout's-honor fashion.

The way his eyes sparked, the way one side of his
mouth curled up in a smile, made her feel as though their
friendship had somehow moved to another level, although
she'd be darned if she knew why it would, why it had.

"Come on," he said. "I'll show you where you'll
be sleeping."

He led her down the hall, and when they passed the
open doorway to a room with a king-size bed and a rum-
pled, forest-green comforter that had been hastily pulled
up, she struggled to keep from slowing her pace, from
peering inside.

Not that she'd snoop or touch anything. It was just
that she missed the masculine scent, the masculine
presence in a house.

She followed Hector to a smaller guest room decorated in pale shades of green and beige. It was as clean
and untouched as a room in a model home. It also
blended nicely with the rest of the house, although the
colors and the fabrics were softer, more feminine.

"I'm going to give you a key to the front door so you
can come and go as you please." He also handed over

his business card. "And this is where you can reach me. If you need anything, give me a call at the office."

"I will."

And for some reason, it wasn't just an automatic response on her part. She would have no qualms about calling him, if she needed to. Hector was proving to be the kind of guy she could rely on, the kind of guy she could...

...fall for?

Easy, she warned herself. Single guys didn't normally date mothers of triplets, especially when the little ones had yet to be born.

A sudden clarity poured over her, and she realized what had been holding her back from telling him that in four months—or perhaps less—she would give birth to three babies.

The news was likely to scare him off.

And she wasn't ready to see him go.

Hector called home once during the day and asked if Samantha needed him to pick up anything on the way home.

"You know," she said, "there's a bakery on Highland Drive that's the best ever. Would you mind stopping by and getting a loaf of French bread?"

"Not at all. Anything else?"

"That'll do it."

"Not even dessert?"

"I've got that covered, too."

When Hector returned home that night and stepped through the door, he was met with the mouthwatering aroma of tomatoes, garlic and basil.

"Something sure smells good," he said as he made his way to the kitchen with the loaf of bread Samantha had asked for.

When he spotted her at the counter, cutting mushrooms to add to a green salad, he couldn't help thinking that it would be nice coming home to one of her dinners each night. And that it would be even nicer coming home to her.

She glanced over her shoulder and offered him a hi-honey-how-was-your-day grin.

If his day had been lousy, seeing her smile would have turned it around in a heartbeat. And if it had been good, seeing her would only make it better.

"I hope you like spaghetti," she said.

"I do. In fact, I love anything Italian, so you'd better make enough for seconds and thirds."

She laughed, and the lilt of her voice nearly bounced off the walls, filling the kitchen with something he could almost touch.

In the past, whenever things got a little too quiet for him, he would call a couple of the partners in the firm and meet them at his favorite sports bar. Or if he just wanted to hang out at the house, he'd invite someone over. But ever since he and Roxanne split, he'd stuck close to home, where his state-of-the-art entertainment center provided the only respite from the silence.

For a while, the solitude had been appealing, but that didn't seem to the be case anymore.

He closed the gap between them, the bakery sack in hand. "Is there something I can do to help?"

"No, I've got everything under control." She took the bread from him, then turned on the oven.

"What about setting the table?" he asked.

"It's already done. But you can butter the bread, if you'd like."

"You got it." He washed his hands, then pulled the loaf out of the plastic bag it had come in and sliced it lengthwise.

"The butter and garlic mixture is in the little red bowl," she said. "And the aluminum foil is next to it. As soon the bread is out of the oven, we can eat."

They stood at the counter, side by side. It felt good to work together, to be together. They'd become a team of sorts.

He slid a glance her way, watched her whip up some vinegar, oil and spices for the dressing.

"I take it you really enjoy entertaining," he said.

"Not for a large group. But cooking dinner is fun, especially tonight. While I was in Europe, I ate every meal out. So it's nice to be able to cook again. And to have someone else to eat with."

Ten minutes later, they were seated at the formal dining table, a fancy piece of furniture the decorator had insisted was perfect. He liked it, even though it had cost a pretty penny. But he hadn't had much use for it before tonight.

Earlier, Samantha had removed the artificial centerpiece and replaced it with a vase of fresh daisies and tapered white candles. He assumed the flowers had come from his backyard, but he'd never seen the crystal bud vase or the candlesticks before.

"Where'd you find these things?" he asked as he twirled the spaghetti onto his fork.

"I brought them from home."

His hand froze, and the strings of the pasta slipped off the tines. "You shouldn't have gone back in that house, Samantha."

"I didn't. I saw the painter while he was taking his lunch break and asked him to get them for me."

They resumed eating, and true to his word, Hector had both seconds and thirds.

As he finally pushed back his plate, he said, "This is the best spaghetti sauce I've ever had."

"I'm glad you like it." She lifted her napkin and blotted her lips. "And by the way, the turkey you're not particularly fond of…?"

"You're kidding."

She smiled. "Surprise!"

"You're full of them, aren't you?"

Their gazes met and held, as sexual awareness stretched between them. At least, that's what it felt like to her. But how could that be happening?

Afraid her imagination had taken off on a tangent again, she broke eye contact and stood to clear the table. "Are you ready for dessert?"

He placed a hand on his stomach. "I wish I wouldn't have had that third helping of spaghetti. Can I wait until my dinner settles?"

"We can pass on it completely."

"There's no need to do that." Hector stood and picked up his plate and utensils. "What are we having?"

"Ice-cream sundaes."

His face brightened. "No kidding? I love ice cream."

She'd figured that out when she peeked into his freezer and saw all the cartons he'd stacked in there.

With Hector's help, they finished the dishes and put the kitchen back in order.

Then they went into the family room, where Hector put a movie into the DVD. "I hope you like action flicks. This one is supposed to have a romance in it, so I figured it was one we'd both enjoy."

They'd just settled onto the sofa, when Samantha's cell phone rang.

"Go ahead and answer it," he said. "I can put the movie on pause."

She glanced at the lighted display of her cell, not recognizing the number. Then she flipped open the phone and lifted it to her ear. "Hello?"

"Samantha?" a female voice said.

"Yes?"

"This is Yolanda Ramirez, Hector's sister. I meant to call earlier today, but one thing led to another, and I just got a chance to catch my breath. I'm not sure what your calendar looks like, but I'd love to meet for lunch one day this week."

"Other than a doctor's appointment on Wednesday, I'm open."

"Good. Then how about Thursday at eleven-thirty?"

"That works for me."

"I'm glad. Why don't we meet at the diner that's across the street from The Green Grocer? Do you know where it is?"

"Yes, I do. Good choice." For some reason, Samantha

didn't want to let Yolanda know where she was right now or who she was with. Had Hector set his sister straight about them yet?

She glanced at Hector and placed a finger to her lips to indicate silence.

The two women made small talk for a moment or two, then after saying goodbye and disconnecting the line, Samantha turned to Hector and smiled. "That was your sister. We're going to get together on Thursday."

"I'm glad you two connected. I think you're going to like each other."

As he reached for the remote to start up the movie again, Samantha's cell rang one more time.

"I'm sorry," she said, reaching back into her purse. "I haven't had a call all day, and now I'm getting them back-to-back."

"No problem."

But this time, when she glanced at the display and recognized the Keatings' number, her heart dropped, and her stomach rolled in a nauseous lurch.

"Do you mind if I take this in the other room?" she asked.

"No, not at all." Yet his brow furrowed, and she felt his eyes on her back while she padded out of the family room.

As she entered the kitchen for some privacy, she answered on the third ring, hoping Marian Keating hadn't hung up yet. "Hi, Marian. What's up?"

"Not much. Randall heard that you're back in the house on Primrose Lane. Is that true?"

"Yes, it is. I moved in on Wednesday and was going

to invite you both over once I got settled. But there's been a lot to do."

Marian didn't respond right away, and Samantha wondered if it was because she wasn't eager to return to the house in which Peter had once lived.

Hoping to steer the subject in another direction and trying to shake an odd niggle of guilt that seemed to have sprung up for no reason at all, Samantha asked, "How have you been?"

"I had a little health scare a couple of months ago. My blood pressure shot up to a dangerous level."

"I'm sorry to hear that."

"It wasn't serious, and it's under control now. So don't worry. How about you, dear? Are you feeling well?"

"I've never felt better." She scanned Hector's kitchen, where she'd spent most of the afternoon, and that niggle of guilt grew stronger.

"That's good to hear. But let me tell you why I called, Samantha. Randall and I will be flying to New York this weekend, but we'd like you to come to dinner a week from Sunday. It's been ages since we've seen you."

Four months, actually. When Samantha had found out she was pregnant, she'd been tempted to tell her in-laws what she'd done, but she hadn't been sure if the implantation would take, and she hadn't wanted to get their hopes up. Then the weeks had turned to months.

"Thanks for the invitation. It'll be nice to see you again." And if it was just going to be the three of them, she could tell them about the babies.

Actually, she realized, as she stroked her distended

belly, she'd have no choice. Her pregnancy would be more than obvious.

"Will you be having any other guests?" Samantha asked.

"Not that I know of, but that could change."

If there's anything Samantha had learned over the past five years, it was that life had a way of changing things—and changing people.

"Well, I hope it doesn't. I'm looking forward to an intimate dinner with you and Randall. It will be nice to catch up."

"Well, thank you, dear. We'd like that, too."

Just to be on the safe side, she would give Marian a call before showing up that day. If there was a change in the guest list and others would be at dinner, Samantha would arrive early and give them the news so they could deal with the surprise privately.

"I'll see you a week from Sunday, then. Thanks for inviting me."

"You're welcome, dear. We miss you. And now that you're closer, we hope to see you more."

For the longest time, Samantha had wanted to fit into the Keating family, and now that she was expecting their three grandchildren, she figured she was well on her way.

Yet she was eager to hang up the phone and return to Hector's family room, where she'd left him waiting for her.

She felt a little uneasy talking to Peter's parents while at Hector's house. She wasn't sure how they'd feel about her new friend. And she had no idea how Hector would feel about them.

As she began to sort through her feelings, the niggle of guilt grew into a fist-size knot.

How odd, she thought. For a moment, she'd sensed that she was cheating on someone, although she wasn't sure who.

Peter?

Or his parents?

Chapter Seven

Halfway through the movie, with Matt Damon in dire straits and the bad guys closing in on him, Hector pushed pause on the universal remote.

"I'm about ready for that ice-cream sundae," he said. "How about you?"

"It sounds good to me." Samantha, who'd been sitting across the sofa from him, got to her feet.

As she started toward the kitchen, he stopped her before she could take two steps. "You don't need to serve me. Wait here, and I'll get mine and bring back a bowl for you."

"But you don't know where I put all the goodies." She nearly leveled him with a pretty smile, and he was toast.

"Okay, but I'm going to help."

As Samantha led the way to the kitchen, she glanced over her shoulder at him. "I'd planned to make a chocolate pound cake for dessert, and then I wondered if you had any vanilla ice cream to go with it."

"That's one thing I never run out of."

She laughed. "I'm sure you don't. Your freezer is packed with more cartons of ice cream than a supermarket."

"What can I say? I'm a kid at heart."

She lobbed him a smile that would have challenged him to a game of tag, if they'd both been kids. But there was nothing the least bit childish about what he was feeling for her right now.

He had an overwhelming urge to flirt, to ask her out to dinner one night soon, and not just because they were neighbors.

But how did a guy go about hitting on a pregnant woman? Just the thought made him shake his head.

After pulling out a can of whipped cream from the fridge, she gathered chocolate sauce, chopped nuts and a jar of cherries on the counter and made a makeshift assembly line.

"Would you look at this?" He ran a hand through his hair as he studied all the sundae fixings. "Where did you get all this stuff? You didn't have it in your bag when you came this morning. I would have noticed."

"That's because when I saw all the Ben & Jerry's in your freezer, I got a craving for homemade sundaes. So I went to the market this afternoon and purchased everything we needed."

"A craving, huh? Did you buy pickles, too?"

"Nope, I'm sorry. I studied all the various brands but couldn't quite bring myself to put a jar into my cart."

"That's a relief."

They both chuckled as they piled scoops of chocolate and vanilla into their bowls.

"Will you pass the whipped cream?" she asked.

"Sure." As he handed her the can of Reddi-wip, he thought of a few other things they could do with the gooey concoction, and none of them had to do with neighbors sharing dinner. But he forced his thoughts on creating a mouthwatering sundae.

He dribbled chocolate over scoops of vanilla, then continued adding the other toppings until he had the perfect dessert.

When Samantha eyed the size of his finished product, she smiled and said, "I guess that means your dinner settled."

"I always have room for ice cream."

They carried their bowls and spoons back into the family room, then took a seat on the sofa. But this time, Samantha sat closer to him than she had before, and he couldn't help reading something into it.

Yet there was the phone call earlier, the conversation she hadn't wanted him to be privy to, even if it was only her side. And he couldn't help thinking the caller must have been a man, which had unsettled him. After all, she'd said that she hadn't dated since Peter died.

On top of that, she'd had in vitro fertilization, which meant she hadn't gotten pregnant the natural way. But that didn't mean she hadn't been involved with someone at least once or twice in the past five years.

He'd assumed that there hadn't been any men in her

life, but he might have been wrong about that. After all, a woman as pretty as Samantha couldn't stay single long.

Hell, he was proof of that. Just look at him. He was tempted to ask her out whenever he looked at her. And each time he heard her laugh or caught a hint of her floral scent, his hormones went wacky.

He could easily imagine making love with her, of caressing the mound of her belly, of taking care to work around it. If he closed his eyes, he could imagine kissing her, stroking her until she cried out in need...

Oh, for Pete's sake, he scolded himself. *Would you just watch the damn movie?*

Focusing on the television screen should have been an easy diversion, since gunshots were ringing out all over the place, and a helicopter with a couple of snipers was swooping in on Matt Damon and an attractive new star Hector had never seen before.

But for some reason, try as he might, Hector couldn't quite lose himself in the story. Not when Samantha was within arm's reach.

Then, to make matters worse, the romantic subplot began to pick up steam. As Matt swept the beautiful blonde into his arms and kissed her deeply, Hector fought the temptation to steal a glance at Samantha and failed.

She'd leaned forward and was nibbling on her bottom lip, apparently caught up in the onscreen romance.

The intensity of her gaze—of her yearning—nearly knocked his breath away, and a rush of heat shot through him.

At that moment, Hector no longer cared about what was happening in the movie. The only romantic subplot that concerned him was the one churning between him and Samantha, and he realized that before her stay with him was over, he was probably going to end up hitting on her.

And the fact that she was expecting a baby didn't matter a bit.

The first thing Bradley Langston had done when the doctor had discharged him from the hospital on Monday was to set up a meeting with Hector on Tuesday morning. So after turning in for the night, Hector had set his alarm for seven, which would give him more than enough time to dress and shower. It would also allow him to spend some time with Samantha in the morning.

Once in his bedroom, he read until nearly eleven, which helped him keep his mind off the fact that Samantha was tucked away just down the hall. Then, after drifting off, he slept like a baby—that is, until Samantha's scream tore through the night.

"No!" she cried out again.

Was she in pain?

He flung off the covers and rolled out of bed. Something terrible must have happened.

She wasn't in premature labor, was she?

He rushed into the hall and hurried to her room.

When he opened the door and flipped on the light, she was sitting upright in bed, the sheets and blankets tangled at her feet. Perspiration had dampened her brow.

"Samantha?" he said. "Honey? Are you okay?"

She raked her fingers through the sleep-tousled

strands of her hair, snagging on a snarl, and turned to him. "Oh, God. I had a nightmare. I'm sorry, Hector."

"That's okay." His adrenaline was pumping like a son-of-a-gun, though, and it would take some time to go back to normal. "I'm glad it was nothing. I was afraid you might have gone into premature labor or something."

He made his way to the bed and sat on the edge of the mattress. "Do you want to tell me about it?"

She blew out shaky sigh. "There's not much to tell. I haven't had a dream like that in ages."

He placed a hand on her shoulder, let it slip slowly to her back. Then he caressed her, offering comfort the only way he knew how. "What was it about?"

"My stepfather used to abuse my mother, and I dreamt about him."

"Did he ever hurt you?"

"No, but he was a real jerk. The first time she tried to leave him, he threatened to kill her if she did it again. And we both believed him."

Hector drew her close, and she rested her cheek against his chin. Her hair brushed across his shoulder, reminding him that he wasn't wearing much—only a pair of boxers.

It didn't seem to bother her, though. Or maybe she hadn't even noticed. Then again, he supposed it didn't matter to either of them.

"I hope your mother eventually left him," Hector said, knowing fear kept many women in abusive relationships.

"She did. And every now and then, I have nightmares about him, about how he used to treat her. Tonight, he was chasing me, telling me that he knew I'd orchestrated her escape, and threatening to kill me."

"Is that true? Were you instrumental in getting your mom to leave him?"

Samantha nodded, yet she remained in his embrace.

"How old were you?"

"Thirteen. I was riding the city bus one day and noticed a poster that provided the phone number for a domestic-abuse hotline. I called on her behalf, and they provided options. I knew we had to leave the house, but he worked from home, so getting away during the daytime was next to impossible. And under normal conditions, he was a light sleeper."

"How'd you manage to escape?"

Samantha lifted her head, and a grin softened the nightmare-induced stress from her face. "What are the statutes of limitation on drugging someone?"

"You drugged him?"

Her gaze sought his, and her smile intensified as a whisper of mischief lit her eyes. "Before I answer that, I need to know if you and I have attorney-client privilege."

Hector broke into a grin. "You bet, honey. Your secret is safe with me."

"The doctor had prescribed anti-anxiety medication for my mom, and there was a warning on the label that said alcohol intensified the effects. So I asked if I could fix dinner that night." She placed her hand on his chest, and his heartbeat kicked up a notch. His breathing, too.

Had she noticed?

"There was a bottle of Chianti in the pantry," she continued, "so I uncorked it to let it breathe."

"You knew how to do that at thirteen?"

"He loved having wine with his meals, especially with pasta. And I'd watched him do it a hundred times."

"So you spiked his drink with the pills?"

"Yes, and as usual, he finished the whole bottle of wine."

"I take it he didn't die."

She shook her head. "I just wanted to buy us some time. So when he passed out, I told her, 'It's now or never.' And we grabbed a few things and hurried out of the house."

"Smart girl," he said, continuing to hold her close, to relish the scent of her floral shampoo. "And you were also brave."

"Thanks." She leaned into him all the more, and he could feel her unwind, relax.

"Did your stepfather ever threaten you?"

"Not really, but hearing him bellow at my mom, watching him beat her, was enough to make me shake in my boots and toe the mark."

"Did you ever hear from him again?"

"No. When we left, we half ran, half walked to the nearest phone booth. I called the people from the shelter, and they picked us up and took us to a safe house. My mom got counseling, and we moved to Hastings. But I have to tell you, we both had a habit of looking over our shoulders for the first couple of years."

"I'm glad you got away."

"Me, too."

Hector sat in the early morning silence, holding Samantha, feeling her softness, her gentle curves, sensing her vulnerability, as well as her courage. He tried to wrap his mind and his heart around all she'd been through, all she'd lost.

And as much as he hated to admit it, he was glad Peter Keating had been able to provide her with a better life, even if he hadn't liked the guy personally.

"I hope your husband showed you that not all men are brutes."

"Peter was a nice guy, and he loved and respected me."

He was nice? Had she loved and respected him back?

Of course she had. She'd married him.

Hector shook off the urge to analyze her words. Instead, he continued to hold her, to bask in the silence punctuated by the tick-tock-tick of the clock on the bureau.

"You know," she said, "I think cooking that spaghetti triggered my nightmare. When I was making the sauce, I remembered the night I slipped those pills into the Chianti."

"Thank goodness I didn't have any wine tonight," Hector said. "That might have really triggered a nightmare."

She pulled away long enough to return his smile. "Thanks for running in here to chase away the bogeyman."

"No problem. Do you think you can go back to sleep now? I could lie down with you for a few minutes if you think it would help."

Her lips parted, and emotion clouded her eyes. He'd be damned if he knew what she was thinking, and about the time he figured her silence meant no, she said, "Actually? I think it *would* help if you stayed with me for a little while."

Hector slowly unwrapped his arms and got to his feet, then waited for her to move into a more comfortable position on the bed. He'd planned to lie down on top of the covers, thinking she might be more comfortable that way considering his barely there attire.

But she drew back the spread and the blankets, and he climbed in with her—without hesitation, which immediately mystified him. They were getting involved deeper and deeper, yet he didn't have any qualms about it.

They lay like that for a while, facing each other. Close enough to touch.

"It's been a long time since I slept with a man," she said. "And I forgot how nice it used to be."

"That's only natural," he said. "We're sexual beings. And you're bound to miss it."

"I'm not talking about making love," she said. "I'm talking about sharing the bed with someone you care about."

"Okay, but don't tell me you don't miss the sex, too."

She sighed. "Yes, I suppose I do."

His ears perked up. She only *supposed* that she missed it?

"The physical part of a marriage is nice, but the best part is having someone to come home to, someone to talk to."

Sex was just *nice?* The conversation was better?

Did that mean her relationship with Peter hadn't been passionate?

Too bad, Hector thought. It sounded as though Peter Keating had dropped the ball—sexually speaking, and Hector couldn't help feeling sorry for her.

In fact, as he lay in bed with her, he couldn't help thinking that someday he'd like to make it up to her, to show her that sex was more than just nice.

That with the right man, it could be…magic.

Samantha slept like a baby.

Around six, she'd awakened in the spoon position, with her bottom pressed against Hector's lap. She could feel the strength of his morning erection through the thin layer of his boxers and her satin gown. Before she knew it, she found herself stirring, too.

She'd felt an almost overwhelming compulsion to roll over, to face him, to run her hand along his cheek, to…start something.

But she'd never been that bold when it came to sex. So she slowly drew away, thinking it might be best to put some distance between them. But as he slept, he pulled her back into his embrace, holding her as though he never wanted to let go.

At least, that's what it seemed like. So she stopped fighting and let herself bask in his touch, in his woodsy scent.

Never had she slept so well, been so safe. Never had she felt such…love?

She'd told him last night that she'd missed having a man in her bed, and that was true. She'd never liked sleeping alone, not after she and her mom had run away from her stepfather.

So as Hector held her in his arms, she fell back asleep, only to wake again at eight-thirty—alone.

The sound of running water suggested that Hector

was in the shower, so she rolled out of bed, then pulled up the sheets and carefully drew up the comforter and replaced the pillows and shams.

After taking the clothes she planned to wear that day, she padded into the bathroom and turned on the spigot and opened the spray. Then she slipped out of her night-gown and let it pool at her feet.

While waiting for her water to warm, she glanced into the mirror, caught the sight of herself naked—the fullness of her breasts, the growing baby bump that seemed to protrude more every day. She liked the ma-ternal image and ran a hand along her belly, fingered the silky skin that stretched over her womb.

Would Hector find her attractive if he were to see her this way?

She couldn't imagine that he would, which was dis-appointing. She was feeling something special for Hector, a spark of passion she hadn't felt for Peter. And last night had only made it stronger.

Of course, there'd been that awkward moment when her phone had rung that second time, and she'd taken the call in private. But how could she talk to Peter's mother while she was having dinner and watching a movie with another man?

She was glad that she'd agreed to stay with Hector rather than in a hotel room, but something told her she could get hurt, and that she'd better watch her step.

Maybe it was time to tell Hector about the triplets, to put in a speed bump sure to slow her runaway thoughts. Once he heard, he'd most likely pull back. Who wouldn't?

So, after taking a shower and shampooing her hair, she dressed for the day and put on a light coat of lipstick. With her hair still damp from the shower, she headed for the kitchen, where she found Hector making coffee.

"Good morning," she said. "I'm usually a light sleeper, so I didn't set an alarm. I just assumed that I would hear you moving around and wake up sooner."

He turned his back to the counter and charmed her with a boyish grin. "I was trying to be quiet. In fact, I didn't want to wake you, so I planned to make a quick cup of coffee to take with me."

"But I'd planned to make breakfast for you," she said.

"Don't worry about me. I'm used to fending for myself."

"You know," she said, "there's something I probably ought to tell you."

"What's that?" He grew serious. "Does it have anything to do with that phone call you received last night?"

"Not exactly."

He crossed his arms and leaned against the kitchen counter. "Then what's up?"

"I told you about the in vitro fertilization."

"Yes. You had it at the Armstrong clinic." He studied her carefully, as if trying to guess what she had to say. "Is something wrong?"

"No. Not at all." Did she dare dump this on him now? As he was leaving?

Hector's gaze grew intense, and she felt as though she was a witness on the stand. "Did the baby's father call you last night?"

"No, he didn't." She wondered why he seemed to

have pounced on that phone call. "I told you the father was out of the picture."

"Then what's with the secrecy?"

"Can we slow down for a moment, Counselor?"

He paused and let his crossed arms unfold and drop to his sides. "I'm sorry. Interrogations have become second nature to me, and that wasn't fair—or necessary. It's none of my business who you talked to last night."

It wasn't as though she was trying to be dishonest or vague. She just hadn't been ready to tell Hector everything yet. "What I'm about to say and that phone call are two separate issues."

Okay, so that explanation wasn't exactly true. Marian Keating and her babies' father were definitely related. But the invitation to the Keatings' house for dinner had nothing to do with anything.

She glanced at him, saw the curiosity etched across his face, but she had to give him credit for biting his tongue and waiting for her explanation.

"I'm pregnant..."

His expression softened. "I know, Samantha. And I'm actually getting used to the idea."

Of her being pregnant? Or of her soon becoming a mother?

But would he ever get used to the idea that she was having three babies in one fell swoop?

There was only one way to find out.

"There's not just one baby, Hector."

His jaw dropped, and his lips parted. "You're having twins?"

"Twins plus one. Two boys and a girl."

"*Three* babies?" His eyes widened, and his jaw dropped lower yet. *"Triplets?"*

She gave a little shrug. "I knew there was a possibility of having multiples, but I was just hoping for one. And…I guess you could say that I got lucky."

At least, she felt lucky. And she hoped Hector saw it that way, too.

"Wow," was all he said.

Triple wow, she thought.

He lifted his arm and glanced at his wristwatch again. "I've got to get out of here. Can we talk about this later?"

What was there to talk about? She was expecting triplets. And any normal guy who wasn't biologically involved—and maybe some who were—would be long gone at the news.

As she heard his footsteps make their way from the house to the garage, as the automatic garage opener went on and the car started up, she realized Hector was long gone already.

Whatever they'd been tiptoeing around, romance or a little harmless flirtation, she was certain had dissipated with the anticipation of three times the diapers, three times the crying, three times the mess.

She had a feeling that when Hector returned from the office today, he'd be cool and distant.

After all, why would he want to get involved with a woman who was having three babies?

Chapter Eight

For a guy who had no trouble thinking on his feet, Hector had been dumbfounded to learn that Samantha was pregnant with triplets. And even if he hadn't been in a rush to leave, he would have been speechless.

Of course, once his thoughts quit spinning, a slew of questions began battering him, like when were the babies going to be born? And how did she plan to raise them alone?

If he hadn't had a ten-o'clock appointment at Langston Construction, and if he hadn't known that it would take him at least an hour to drive across town during morning rush hour, he might have stuck around the house a little longer. He could have called the office and told them he was coming in late. But Bradley

Langston didn't like to be put off. And he'd been champing at the bit to have this meeting.

Still, Hector had thought long and hard about Samantha and her plight on the drive to Langston's office.

She was really going to have her hands full when the babies came. Who in the world would help her?

He supposed she could hire a nanny, but something told him she would want to take a hands-on approach and raise the children herself. And if that were the case, he had no doubt that she'd do a good job of it.

The morning meeting went into overtime, with Langston finally admitting that he might have flirted a little with the former employee who was now suing the corporation for sexual harassment. And then he'd added that he might have jokingly asked her to spend the weekend with him in Atlantic City.

As Langston droned on about being a victim, Hector began to suspect the young woman had a solid case, and he strongly suggested they try to settle out of court. The board of directors was inclined to agree, but Langston wanted to fight it, saying his former employee misunderstood his intent.

"If you want to fight this thing to convince your wife that you're true blue," Hector said, "tell her that your attorney advised against it. And that the board wanted to keep the cost of litigation down, since the legal fees could skyrocket. Then, if you're that concerned about saving your marriage, take her on a second honeymoon. How about a cruise? A trip like that might do your health some good, too."

"But who's going to run things around here if I leave?" Langston had argued.

"Oh, hell," the vice-president of operations snapped. "What are we? Office fixtures? Take your wife to the Mediterranean. She's a good woman, Brad. And she doesn't deserve the embarrassment or the grief."

Langston had reluctantly agreed, then buzzed his secretary and asked her to book them the best cabin available on the Crystal cruise line—ASAP.

After the meeting ended, Hector returned to the office just in time to check his messages, return phone calls and grab a bite to eat at the corner deli, where they made a great roast beef and cheddar sandwich.

While he was seated at one of the café-style tables near the front window, he glanced across the tree-lined street and noticed an antique shop that displayed several pieces of furniture out front. One of them was a wooden rocking chair.

It reminded him a lot of the one his mom used to have, one she had his father bring down from the attic when Yolanda had first announced she was expecting.

"*Mija,* you have no idea how handy that chair is going to be," his mom had said. "Or how comfortable it is. They just don't make chairs like this anymore. It used to belong to my grandmother, and she gave it to me. I rocked each of you kids in it."

Yolanda had gotten all teary-eyed, and the women had hugged. Later, Yolanda told Hector that the gifting of the chair had been a special mother/daughter moment.

Heirlooms aside, he realized that Samantha wouldn't be having any of those mother/daughter moments.

So, after wolfing down his sandwich, Hector carried his soda across the street to get a closer look at the rocker on display. He even sat in it to make sure it was sturdy, yet comfortable.

"How much do you want for that old chair out in front?" he asked the shopkeeper.

"Three hundred dollars, but I'll take off ten percent for cash."

Hector couldn't believe he was asking so much. What would a new chair cost?

"That's a lot of money for a used rocker," he said.

"No, it's not. That chair was handcrafted before the Civil War, and it's in good condition."

Hector pondered the purchase a moment longer, then reached into his wallet and peeled out three one-hundred dollar bills.

After getting a receipt, he picked up the chair and carried it back to the office. Once he got home, he would surprise Samantha with it. He figured, with three babies, she'd get three times the use out of it.

Of course, a brand-new rocker might have been a more practical gift, since he hadn't noticed a single antique in her house, but it looked so much like the one Yolanda had.

And for some lame reason, Hector wanted to give Samantha a special moment, too.

All day long, Samantha had been uneasy. And now, as it neared five o'clock, she was waiting for Hector to return from work.

She had a feeling that their relationship had taken a big turn this morning, and not in a good direction. She'd cooked dinner for two, but if he acted the least bit distant, she was going to check into a hotel.

Of course, if the thoughts she'd had about romance were only one-sided, and if, as he'd said, he was only trying to be neighborly, then her having three babies instead of one wouldn't bother him a bit.

At ten minutes after five, she picked up the newspaper he'd left on the kitchen table and carried it into the living room. Then she took a seat near the window, in the warmth of the setting sun as it shined through the glass.

She was reading an article about a fashion show luncheon and an auction that would benefit the local women's shelter. Halfway through, she decided to not only attend but to offer her financial support, as well. She'd just found a contact number, when she heard Hector's car drive up.

She tried her best to look cool, calm and collected, but when he walked into the house carrying a beat-up old rocking chair and banging the spindled backrest against the doorjamb, she couldn't help but stare at him.

"What's that?" she finally asked.

"A rocker."

"I realize that, but what are you doing with it?"

"I'm giving it to you."

She folded the newspaper, set it upon the glass-top coffee table and got to her feet. "For me? I don't understand."

"It's an antique. And I thought it was kind of interesting. I know it just looks like something you'd find at a garage sale, but it was handcrafted in the early nineteenth century. It's really comfortable. You ought to try it out."

When it came to giving and receiving gifts, Samantha's mother had always insisted that it was the sentiment behind the gift that held the most value. And Hector's thoughtfulness touched her beyond measure.

"You don't like it," he said as he continued to stand in the middle of the room.

"No, that's not it. I'm just…surprised, that's all. Where did you get it?"

"At an antique store not far from my office."

She ran her hand along the carved backrest, then set the chair in motion.

"My grandmother used to have a rocker like that," he added, "and she gave it to my mother a couple of months before I was born. And just recently, my mom passed it down to Yolanda, who was thrilled to get it. So I thought…"

"I don't know what to say, Hector."

His smile faltered. "I just picked it up on a whim. It's no big deal. I can take it back if you don't like it. I've got the receipt."

"Oh, but I *do* like it." And as far as she was concerned, it was a very big deal. Besides, it was the first baby gift she'd received.

She took a seat in the chair, rested her hands on the armrests and proceeded to rock back and forth.

"I know this isn't an heirloom, like the one my sister has. And since you don't know the original owner, there's no sentimental value attached to it."

He was wrong, Samantha thought. There was a great deal of sentiment in the gift. And she'd been touched by the man who'd given it to her.

"You have no idea how much I appreciate this, Hector. When my mom and I escaped from my stepdad that night, we only packed a few clothes and whatever we could carry. We had to leave everything else behind—photographs, jewelry my real father had given her, even the old family Bible, with the names and birth dates of my great-grandparents. So you can be sure this rocker will have a place of honor in my house."

"You can have it refinished," he said. "It would look good with a new stain and varnish. Or you could even paint it to match the colors in the nursery."

"It also has charm and character, so I just might leave it as it is."

"That's up to you."

She stopped the chair's motion, got to her feet and faced him. "Thanks for thinking about me. It's a wonderful gift."

Then she gave him an appreciative hug, letting their contact linger, absorbing his warmth and strength, relishing his woodsy scent. She melded into him, much like she'd done last night when she'd had the nightmare and he'd come running to her rescue.

She would have let go, would have stepped away, if he'd given her a sign that he thought it had gone on long enough, but he continued to hold her, as if he was breathing her in, too. As if his feelings were evolving into something that matched her own, something powerful and lasting.

As she finally released her arms from around him, she looked into his eyes, caught an emotion she couldn't quite grasp.

Whatever it was set her heart thumping, her hope soaring, but she was afraid to read too much into it.

Instead, she said, "You have no idea how glad I am that we've become friends."

"Just friends?"

Her eyes widened, and her breath stalled. "Are we becoming more than that?"

"I don't know." He lifted his hand, skimmed his knuckles along her cheek. "I really have no idea what's going on, Samantha."

Apparently, the triplets hadn't scared him off, which thrilled her beyond measure. Like him, she really wasn't sure where this was going, but she liked whatever she was feeling—a lot.

Trouble was, she still couldn't bring herself to tell him that the babies were Peter's.

And she wasn't sure why.

Just moments ago, Hector had come very close to pulling Samantha back into his arms and kissing her senseless. But good sense—or maybe just plain masculine fear—had held the temptation in check.

He hadn't expected her to thank him for the chair by giving him a hug, but he'd relished her touch, as well as the warmth of her body and the whisper of peppermint on her breath.

The silky strands of her hair had brushed against his cheek, and the floral scent of her shampoo had taunted him. The gentle curves of her body, even the swell of her belly, had fit perfectly into his embrace.

He would have expected just the opposite to be

true—that the bulge of her pregnancy might get in the way and make things awkward. But it hadn't, and if she hadn't slowly removed her arms and stepped back, God only knew how long he might have held on to her.

Their embrace hadn't seemed to affect her in the same way it had him. Or maybe it had. She'd seemed a little unbalanced, a little uneasy.

When she'd told him how glad she was that they'd become friends, he hadn't been able to let that statement go without comment. Still, he'd be damned if he knew just what they'd become, but certainly more than just neighbors, more than friends.

As they'd stood there, close enough to touch again, to kiss, he'd stroked her cheek, and everything that had been brewing between them had risen to the surface, demanding to be acknowledged. Still, he wasn't exactly sure what it was or what to do about it.

He'd admitted that much, which was a pretty big step for him in and of itself—even if she'd only been expecting one baby.

Now, as she looked at him, and those pretty blue eyes filled with an unidentifiable emotion, she was only a step and a simple reach away. But he couldn't quite go that far and decided to put some distance between them, at least until he could wrap his mind around what he was feeling, what he was willing to risk.

He reached for the back of the rocker. "Why don't I take this over to your house for you and put it away. And while I'm there, I can also check on the painter's progress."

Maybe she craved the distance, too, because she said, "That's a good idea. Thanks, Hector. I'd appreciate that."

"Is there anything you'd like for me to get while I'm over there?" he asked.

She pondered his offer for a moment, then brightened. "I bought a book the other day and left the bag in the backseat of my car." She went to her purse, pulled out a set of house keys and handed them to him. "The car is in the garage."

"No problem. Is that all?"

"For now." She offered him a breezy smile that made him sorry he was leaving, sorry that he wasn't going to wait it out and see what developed between them.

"I'll have dinner on the table when you get back," she said.

He nodded, then picked up the rocker and headed for the door. Once outside, he carried it down his walkway, then cut across the lawn to her yard. After letting himself into her house, the smell of paint accosted him, and he was glad she'd moved out until the odor faded.

Deciding to check out the painter's work first, he left the rocker in the living room and walked through the house, scanning the walls, all of which had been masked and prepared. The man seemed to have gotten a lot done today, but Hector guessed that he had a couple of days' work left. The nursery, though, with its bright blue walls and white trim, was almost finished. The only thing missing was the wallpaper.

He tried to envision it with the farm print on the walls, with three cribs, three dressers. Three babies.

Samantha's life would be changing big-time in a few months. Did he want to be a part of it?

He imagined coming home to Samantha, to the

babies, and he found himself saying yes. But maybe it was best if he took it one day at a time.

So he left the nursery, headed for the kitchen and the door that led to the garage. Once inside, he flipped on the light switch and immediately spotted the white Jag—how could he miss it? But he also noticed that the stacks of boxes she'd designated for the Salvation Army were still there.

She'd told him they were filled with Peter's belongings and mentioned that she was going to have someone come and pick them up. Had she forgotten to make the call? Or was she dragging her feet on purpose? Maybe, subconsciously, she was trying to hold on to the man and his memory.

After five years, one would think that she would be able to move on with her life. But maybe she hadn't.

Hector made his way to the Jag and found the shopping bag in the backseat, just as she'd said he would. He peered inside and checked out the book she'd bought: *What to Expect When You're Expecting.*

He thumbed through it for a moment, realizing she was definitely looking toward the future.

Good, he thought. The babies would give her plenty on which to focus. So if she had any lingering thoughts about the past and Peter, they'd fall by the wayside soon enough.

He certainly hoped so, because he wouldn't play second fiddle to a ghost.

When Hector returned to his house with the shopping bag, he found Samantha in the kitchen, preparing a tossed salad.

She stopped what she was doing and turned to face

him, resting her hip against the counter. "So, how does the nursery look? I asked him to start in there."

"He did a good job. I think you're going to like the color, as well as the white trim. Once the wallpaper goes up, you should be happy with it."

"I can't wait to see it."

They stood across the room from each other, a new conversation unfolding. Still, he couldn't quite shake the one they'd had before, the one in which he'd admitted to feeling something for her. But he really needed to think things through, to take things one day at a time, no matter how he was beginning to feel.

"Is there anything I can do to help?" he asked. "Maybe set the table?"

"No. Most of the work was done before I went for my walk. So once I finish this salad, we can eat."

Minutes later, they were seated in the dining room, where they enjoyed a tasty meal of baked chicken, rice pilaf and salad. All the while, they made small talk. At least, he might have considered it small talk in the past, but he'd really liked hearing what she'd done today, about an article she'd read. And he'd enjoyed sharing a bit about one of the cases his firm was representing, too.

But by the time she'd served a fruit tart for dessert, he couldn't help making a comment about Peter's belongings.

"I notice you've still got those boxes in the garage."

She lifted her fork from the table. "Oh, yeah. I forgot all about that. I need to call the Salvation Army tomorrow and find out when their truck will be in the neighborhood."

"I can drop them off for you on my way to the office tomorrow."

"I hate to have you do that."

"It's no trouble at all." He cut into the tart with his fork and speared a big, gooey bite.

"Are you sure?" she asked.

"Absolutely." He'd be glad to get rid of anything that would trigger her memory of Peter.

After all, she was starting a new life.

And, at least for the time being, Hector couldn't help wanting to be the only man in it.

Chapter Nine

Yolanda and Samantha met for lunch at Delano's, a trendy sidewalk café that was located across the street from The Green Grocer. The weather was as nice as any other late-spring day, so they asked for one of the outdoor tables that faced the street.

They each ordered the grilled chicken salad and iced herbal tea. Then, while they waited for their food, they enjoyed the chance to talk and get to know each other.

"So," Yolanda said, "when is your due date?"

"October 10."

"Are you kidding?" Her brow furrowed, and her eyes narrowed. "That means you're only four-and-a-half months along. And you're way too big for that." As if realizing her response might have been taken the wrong way, she added, "I'm sorry, Samantha. I don't mean that badly. It's just that there's got to be some mistake. Are you sure you're not farther along than that? Have they checked you for twins?"

"Actually, I had a sonogram more than a month ago, and they did check for twins."

"And what did they find?"

"Three babies. I'm going to have triplets."

"Wow." Silence welled between them as Yolanda took it all in. Then she seemed to get it all together. "Triplets? That's awesome, although I have to admit, I'm thinking better you than me. I don't know what I'd do with three newborns." Yolanda broke into a grin. "Does my brother know?"

"I told him yesterday." Samantha lifted her glass of tea and took a sip.

Yolanda's lips parted as though there was another question on the tip of her tongue, but if so, she reeled it back in.

"I know it won't be easy," Samantha said, "but I'm really looking forward to having them and bringing them home. My house has been incredibly quiet for the past five years, longer than that, even. So I can't wait to hear the patter of little feet."

Yolanda chuckled. "That ought to be a big change for my brother."

"What do you mean?"

"He told me that you two were friends, but you seem to be spending a lot of time together for that."

So Hector's sister had connected the dots and come to a logical conclusion. But Samantha wasn't ready to admit that they were more than friends. They were still tiptoeing around their feelings, and the jury was still out on that.

"My house is being painted," she said. "So rather than get a hotel room, your brother offered to let me stay with him—in his guest room."

Of course, they'd technically slept in the same bed, but that wasn't the same.

Or was it? They'd certainly shared an intimacy, even if they hadn't made love. They hadn't even kissed. But if heated looks and caresses counted...

"I'm sorry," Yolanda said. "I didn't mean to imply you two couldn't be friends or that things might not be platonic between you. It's just that I'm a romantic at heart."

"Aren't most women matchmakers?"

"Maybe. But I think I have a tendency to go overboard. My brother accused me of have having a Noah syndrome."

"Oh, yeah?" Samantha had heard of the Peter Pan syndrome. "What's that?"

Yolanda laughed. "Hector probably coined the term himself, but he said I wasn't happy unless people were going through life two by two."

"I can see the benefit of that. Life can certainly be lonely at times."

"That's why I'm trying to see my brother hook up with someone. He's been alone for nearly six years. Not that he doesn't date. But he seems to keep women at arms' distance, and I think that's because his ex-wife hurt him."

"How so?"

"She married him knowing his career was a priority, and that he loved his work. Then she complained about how much time he spent at the office, how driven he was. But she didn't have any complaints about the money he earned."

"Apparently it didn't work out," Samantha said, connecting her own dots.

"Whatever physical attraction they'd had wasn't strong enough to survive their problems. Hector's dedication to the firm paid off when he was made a partner, but it had a negative effect on his marriage. Patrice got tired of his long hours away from home, and just before their second anniversary, she asked for a divorce."

"Was Hector okay with the split?"

"He felt badly about it, since he'd never failed at anything in his life, but he poured himself into his work. He told me once that he wasn't cut out for marriage, but I don't think that's true."

They continued to pick at their salads until Samantha asked, "What was Hector like as a little boy?"

"He was the typical firstborn. And he set a high benchmark for me and Diego, our younger brother. But then again, so did our parents."

"In what way?"

"My mom and dad were immigrants, and when they moved to this country, they were determined to work hard and to share in the American dream. So as kids, we were encouraged to do our best in school. We all did well academically, but Hector was especially bright. Eventually, he received scholarships, graduated from college with honors and went to law school."

"What about you?" Samantha asked.

"I'm a schoolteacher—fourth grade."

"And Diego?"

"He has a contractor's license and owns his own company."

So they'd each succeeded, Samantha realized. "I hope I get a chance to meet your brother and your parents someday. They sound like good people."

Yolanda took a bite of her salad, then paused. "Hey, I've got an idea. I'll plan a taco fest and a family game night one of these days."

"What's that?"

"Just an excuse to get together and eat some of the food we grew up on and have a few laughs. I'll check my calendar when I get home, then give Hector a call to invite him. I'll tell him to bring you, too."

"Sounds like fun."

While they waited for the bill, Yolanda said, "I hope you and Hector will be able to join us for dinner one night soon. I know he works a lot, but he really needs to take a break on weekends." Then she clicked her tongue. "Boy, I sound just like Patrice, don't I?"

His ex-wife, Samantha realized.

Yolanda lifted her napkin to her lips. "I don't mean to give him a hard time. I'm really proud of him. He's built a reputation for defending big corporations in environmental cases."

Uh-oh. Peter had done what he could to protect the environment against corporations.

Samantha wondered if that's what had caused the rift between the two men. It seemed possible, since Hector had said they had different world views.

It would probably be in her best interests to learn the details about the trouble Hector and Peter once had.

And then she could convince Hector that her late husband had been a good man, that he'd rescued her and had treated her with the utmost respect.

"The biggest case my brother ever defended was about five years ago, shortly after he bought his house."

"Oh, really?" Peter had been caught up in a big case at that time, too.

"He was representing a huge corporation who'd been responsible for an oil spill that leaked into the water table and contaminated a river. A group of environmentalists began a protest of the company, marching in the streets and blocking people from driving in and out of the parking lot."

Samantha vaguely remembered hearing about a case like that.

"One of the protesters set fire to a building belonging to the corporation, and a night janitor was killed."

Now it was really sounding familiar. Peter had mentioned something about it, saying the arsonist had some mental problems and that he'd been a loose cannon.

"Hector really took that case to heart, in part because the CEO was a self-made man. He also sympathized with the family of the janitor, who was a Mexican immigrant and the father of four young children."

According to Peter, the arsonist wasn't actually connected to the group; he'd just decided to help further the cause.

"Hector blamed the entire group, as well as their financial backer."

"Do you know who that was?" Samantha asked.

"No, I really didn't follow the case, but the guy with the money was killed in a car accident, which weakened the case against the corporation. And Hector and his firm managed to win the judgment."

Samantha paled, and her stomach clenched. That had to be it. That must be the reason behind the rift. And if her suspicion was right, would Hector hold that against her? Against the babies?

Of course, he wouldn't. She'd seen a side of Hector this past week that she'd never expected—especially after Peter had called him a jerk and suggested they steer clear of him.

"Enough of that," Yolanda said.

Of what? Pondering what the men had said or done that had caused them to dislike and distrust each other?

"I'm sorry," Samantha said, thinking she might have missed something. "Enough of what?"

"Singing my brother's praises. His success speaks for itself. Let's just say my family and I are proud of him."

"I'm sure you are." Samantha smiled at her new friend, then glanced at her watch. "Well, I'd better go. I need to pick up groceries on the way home. I'm fixing pot roast tonight."

"For two?"

Samantha laughed. "Boy, your brother was right. You *do* have the Noah syndrome."

"I guess that wasn't any of my business."

"Probably not, but that's okay. I'm fixing dinner at Hector's house, and we're eating together."

"You don't say?" Yolanda brightened. "He must really care about you."

"He's been very nice to me, but there really isn't anything between us." Not yet, anyway.

"Are you sure about that?" Yolanda asked.

Not really. When it came to her feelings for Hector, she wasn't sure about anything these days.

Did she dare admit that they were growing close, that they were feeling something for each other, even if they hadn't quite figured out what it was?

No, not yet. Not to Hector's sister.

So she said, "At this point, I've got way too much going on in my life to even think about romance."

"I know." Yolanda turned and removed the shoulder strap of her purse from the back of her chair. "But the babies will be here before you know it."

"You're right about that. But then I'll have even less time for romance."

"Yes, but you'll also have more need for someone special in your life."

The truth of that statement stretched between them until Samantha said, "I'm going to have to take one day at a time."

"And you're smart to do that." Yolanda pushed her chair away from the table and stood. "But you can't blame me for hoping that things work out between the two of you."

Samantha found herself hoping the same thing, which was why she planned to keep the identity of the babies' father a secret for a little while longer.

Then, after Hector got used to the idea of her having three babies, he might not even give genetics a single thought.

After lunch, Samantha had planned to stop at The Green Grocer since it was just across the street from the café. She needed to pick up some milk and sugar, as well as potatoes and a rump roast. But she also had some other shopping to do and an errand to run. And since she didn't want the food to spoil if she left it in the car, she set the grocery list aside and drove to Pretty Mama, a trendy store that catered to expectant mothers.

While scanning the racks of summer dresses, she chatted with one of the salesclerks. She also met a woman who'd just learned that she was expecting twins. So she ended up spending more time at Pretty Mama than she'd planned—and more money, too, since she found a sundress, two tops and a pair of shorts that she liked.

All in all, it had been a lovely afternoon, but if she didn't get that roast into the oven, it wouldn't be ready in time for dinner.

So she made a quick stop at the post office, then went back to the market. She'd no more than chosen a small rump roast, when her cell phone rang. It was Hector.

"How was lunch?" he asked.

She smiled at the sound of his voice and found herself amused by his curiosity. It must be nice to be a close-knit family, to care about one's siblings.

"Lunch was great," she said. "I had a good time."

"You can tell me all about it when I get home. I have a couple of clients waiting for me in the conference room, so I can't talk now. But I wanted to tell you not to cook tonight."

She glanced at the rump roast she'd just put in her cart. "Why not?"

"Because I thought it would be nice to grill. We can eat outside on the patio. What do you say?"

She couldn't remember the last time she'd eaten outside, and it sounded like fun. "Would you like me to make a salad and baked potatoes?"

"If you want to. I don't mind picking up a container of coleslaw or potato salad so you can have a break from cooking."

She scrunched up her nose; she hated ready-made convenience food. "I don't need a break. Let me worry about the side dishes."

"Deal. But I've got to run, Sam. I'll see you around five-thirty."

As the line disconnected, she continued to hold her cell phone without putting it away.

He'd called her Sam, the nickname her mother had given her. And she found it touching, since Peter had always been more formal.

Was calling her Sam a sign that their—what? friendship? relationship?—was becoming more intimate?

Stop, she scolded herself. He was in a hurry, so he'd clipped the entire conversation. Besides, friends oftentimes had nicknames for each other.

She put away her cell, then looked at the roast, thinking she might as well buy it, anyway. She could always freeze it and fix it another night.

After stopping in the produce aisle, she headed for the checkout lanes, then got into the car and drove home. Well, not to *her* house. She drove to Hector's.

Once she put everything away, she read her new pregnancy book for a while. Then she watched a little television—a *Touched By An Angel* rerun. If she'd been at her house, she would have found any number of projects to tackle. But she couldn't very well clean out Hector's closets or garage for him.

At four-thirty, she decided to get some exercise by walking in the neighborhood. It had been a pleasant afternoon so far, and even more so now that the shadows had grown long and a scatter of birds chirped overhead.

She arrived back home just as Hector returned, and her heart skipped a beat.

He climbed from his car with a grocery bag. He tossed her a smile that nearly turned her inside out, and she fumbled to return it.

"What are you doing?" he asked.

"I went for a walk."

He clicked on the key remote and locked his car door, then joined her on the sidewalk. "How does your doctor feel about that? Aren't you supposed to be taking it easy?"

His concern was touching. "Walking is good for me. And yes, this is considered a high-risk pregnancy. But everything is progressing as well as can be expected. The babies will probably come early, and there are other complications that can arise, but I've got a good doctor—one of the best in the country. And he's monitoring me closely."

"Good." As they both turned and strode toward the house, Hector added, "So, tell me about lunch."

"The food was good, and your sister was really nice. I like her."

Hector opened the door for her, and she stepped inside.

"Your sister is also going to invite us to her house for a taco fest and game night one of these days."

"Are you sure you're up for something like that?"

It didn't sound wacky or rowdy to her. "What do you mean?"

"Meeting my family."

"Sure. Why not?"

He didn't say, and she wondered if she should be concerned, if maybe he had qualms about taking her to meet them.

As they entered the kitchen, she decided to give him an easy way out. "We certainly don't have to go if you're not up for it."

"I'm okay with going." He placed the grocery sack on the counter. "My family is great. You'll like them, and I'm sure they'll like you."

Still, if he'd looked her in the eye when he'd said that, she'd have felt better. So she faced the truth head-on. "You seem a little hesitant, which is fine. Really."

He turned toward her, and their gazes locked. Something simmered in his warm, brown eyes, something heart-stirring and breath-catching.

She couldn't gauge the distance between them, since the intensity in his gaze seemed to connect them. Still, he stepped toward her, narrowing whatever gap there was.

When they were just a whisper apart, he lifted his hands and cupped her jaw. His thumbs brushed against her cheek. "It's just that you'll be on display, Sam. Every single one of them is going to think that we're an item, and that your babies are probably mine."

And that was a bad thing?

He must have sensed her confusion, her worry, because he brushed a kiss on her brow, then dropped his hands and returned to what he'd been doing. With his back to her again, he reached into the sack and pulled out the meat.

His kiss stunned her. She could have joined him at the counter, but for some reason, her feet didn't move. Her hand did, and she trailed her fingers along her cheek, on the spot that still tingled from his touch.

Had they become an "item"?

She'd be darned if she knew.

So how in the world could she blame his family for wondering?

Hector had gotten a late start on grilling the meat, thanks to one interruption after another.

While the steaks marinated, he'd taken a shower and slipped into some comfortable clothing—cargo shorts and a T-shirt. He'd returned to the kitchen, only to find that Samantha had made herself scarce. Or maybe it had just seemed that way, since he kissed her. Not that the kind of kiss you'd give an elderly aunt or a toddler counted. But it had come from the heart—sweet and unexpected—so he wasn't sorry.

At six o'clock, he'd gone outside to heat the barbecue and to set the table. But he'd gotten a phone call from one of the newer attorneys at the firm about a wrongful-death suit that could prove to be a big one—and high-profile. So he'd gone into the den, where he could speak privately.

The attorney wanted his advice, and after getting the details and sharing his initial thoughts, Hector had called another one of the partners for a second opinion. By the time they'd all settled on a solid game plan, it was nearly dark when he'd started to grill the meat.

Now he and Samantha sat at a candlelit table, their plates full. His wine goblet was filled with cabernet sauvignon, and hers with milk.

The moon was new, and the stars were sparkling bright in the night sky. Indoors, the stereo played soft music, a perfect touch to the evening meal.

"I'm sorry I took so long on that phone call," he said.

"That's okay. I kept the potatoes warm."

As they ate in silence, Hector couldn't help thinking that the last few meals he'd shared with Samantha had been some of the nicest he'd had in years, and not just because of the taste of the food.

Maybe it was because of the company, he thought as he glanced across the table at his pretty dining companion.

She was wearing a pale blue sundress that did the most amazing thing to the color of her eyes, especially in the candlelight. Her hair was curled along her shoulders, and he wondered if she'd fixed it just for him.

Whether she had or not, Hector couldn't keep his eyes off her.

"It's a beautiful night," she said, glancing at the sky. "The temperature is perfect. Can you believe that we had such a cold and rainy evening last week?"

No, he couldn't. But he found it even more difficult to believe that he'd actually taken off early today— something he rarely did—just because he'd wanted to come home to Samantha.

Not willing to make an admission like that, he said, "The weather can be a little unpredictable at this time of year." And that was true. But then again, ever since

Samantha had moved back to Primrose Lane, he'd found a lot of things hard to second-guess. Like his growing attraction to his pregnant neighbor.

In the background, Eric Clapton sang a love song, and Hector couldn't help thinking that the words were perfect. Because Samantha certainly looked wonderful tonight.

But it was more than her appearance that drew him to her, and he had a feeling that he could easily fall in love with her—if he'd let himself.

They continued to eat in silence, and when they'd finished, Hector reached for the wine bottle and poured a second glass for himself. Moments later, Samantha stood and began to gather her place setting.

"I'll get that later," he said. "Why don't you sit out here with me for a while. It's such a nice night."

"I thought I'd get another glass of milk, so it seemed like a good idea to carry in the plates while I was at it."

"Then let me help."

They cleared the table, then took the dirty dishes to the kitchen. Hector waited while Samantha filled her goblet with milk, then they walked outside together.

"I can't believe how clear and bright everything is tonight." Samantha arched her neck and scanned the sky. "Look at the moon. It's so full. And the stars are so twinkly."

Hector glanced up, but he was more interested in watching Samantha—and thank God that he was.

While looking at the sky instead of her path, she stumbled, dumping half the milk from her glass and nearly taking a tumble.

He grabbed her and held her close. "Are you all right?" He sure hoped so. What would happen if she tripped and fell in her condition?

"I'm okay," she replied, looking down at her feet, then at his grip on her arm. "But that was a close one."

As her face lifted and her eyes met his, something—the summer sky, the evening breeze, the attraction that had been sparking over them since she'd moved back into the neighborhood—surged between them.

Hector had ignored the stirrings for as long as he could, but he was only human. With his heart racing, his pulse thundering, his hormones rushing through his veins, he tilted her chin and lifted her lips to his.

The kiss was soft, tentative, like that of two teenage lovers experimenting with love and passion for the very first time. But as she leaned into him, as her lips parted, inviting him to take the lead, he was lost.

Their breaths mingled, their hearts pounded and their tongues dipped and tasted until the tender kiss exploded with heat.

As Hector drew her closer, glass shattered on the concrete, and he realized the goblet had slipped from her hands.

"Oh, no," she said as she broke the kiss. "I'm sorry about that."

About the broken glass? Or about the kiss?

He wanted to tell her to hell with the goblet. He'd rather lower his mouth to hers again and forget the broken glass. But he figured it was better to get his mind grounded in reality, rather than…whatever they were doing.

"It's no big deal," he said. "Don't worry about it, Sam."

He carefully maneuvered her a couple of steps away from the mess, yet he didn't release her. Instead, he placed his forehead against hers and continued to hold her close, breathing in her floral scent. "So, where do we go from here?"

"I have no idea." She slowly drew away from his embrace and rested one hand on the mound of her belly, reminding him that she wasn't the kind of woman a man could kiss on a whim.

There was too much waiting in the wings. But he shook it all off—the heated kiss that had knocked him senseless, as well as the fact that their relationship had just kicked up a notch on the intimacy scale—just as he'd tried to shake off the mess on the ground.

"I'll clean this up," he said, "why don't you pour yourself another glass?"

"Actually," she said. "I think I've had enough for tonight."

Enough of what? Kissing him? He wasn't sure he wanted an answer to that, but he said, "It was just a kiss."

"I know. But it packed a powerful punch."

It certainly had. "So what do you want to do about it?"

"Nothing. Something. I don't know."

Well, that made two of them. He nodded toward the table where the candle still flickered, where his wine waited. "Have a seat. We can talk more about it when I get back. I'll just be a minute."

"You know, I think I'd rather help you pick up this mess and do the dishes so I can turn in for the night."

"Are you all right?" he asked.

"I'm fine." She offered him a smile he found impossible to read. *"Really."*

But something told him neither of them would be "fine" again.

Chapter Ten

Hector's kiss had not only swept Samantha off her feet, but her reaction to it had knocked her for a loop.

The gentle assault of his lips had escalated from sweet and tender to heated and demanding, which had weakened her knees. Within heartbeats, she'd been filled with an overwhelming need for more.

He'd said it was just a kiss, and maybe he was right. But by the time she'd turned in for the night and had climbed into bed, she'd realized that it had been much more than that to her.

She'd lain awake for the longest time, trying to sort through her thoughts and feelings. Eventually, she'd dozed off, but she was up again just after dawn.

Realizing she'd better call it a night, she climbed out of bed and headed for the shower.

Now, as a spray of warm water poured over her head, she reached for the bottle of shampoo, squirted a dab into her hand and lathered her hair. But rather than gaining some clarity, her thoughts again drifted to the questions that plagued her.

What would have happened if she'd moved back to Primrose Lane before visiting the Armstrong Fertility Institute, before the in vitro? Would she have gone ahead with the pregnancy plan? Or would she and Hector have…?

There it went again, the start of another replay of all the what-ifs that had crossed her mind last night.

She rinsed the shampoo from her hair, climbed from the shower and grabbed a towel. She paused long enough to run her hand along her swollen belly. Each day, it seemed, the babies were growing bigger, making her baby bump more pronounced. And she realized this wasn't about Hector and it wasn't about her. The babies were her top priority.

Don't worry, she silently whispered to her little ones. *It's the hormones, that's all. I love you all very much, and I'm thrilled to have you.*

She dried off, then began to slip into her underwear and the new sundress she'd purchased yesterday.

It was only a kiss, Hector had said, downplaying it all. But that had been some kiss.

And he was some man.

And she was…

Sudden awareness swept over her, and she realized that she was falling for him. And where did that leave her?

She blew out a sigh. But worse than that, where would

she be if her feelings were only one-sided? What if Hector had been brutally honest when he'd said that the kiss they'd shared hadn't been anything out of the ordinary?

As she ran a brush through her wet hair, she told herself to get a grip on the crush she had on Hector.

Maybe she should have told him that she was carrying Peter's children last night. That certainly would have put a damper on her fantasies. But for some reason—the moon, the stars, the heart-spinning smiles of the handsome man seated across from her—she hadn't wanted to ruin the magic.

Nevertheless, she was going to have to tell him—and soon. Maybe even over breakfast.

As she reached for the blow-dryer and plugged it in, she realized that telling him wasn't going to be easy.

How did she slip the news into the conversation? *Oh, funny you should mention the babies, Hector. Did I tell you that they're Peter's children?*

Would he back off? Be less likely to want to be a part of her life, the triplets' lives? Would he wonder why she hadn't told him right from the get-go?

She blew out a sigh, then styled her hair and applied a bit of lipstick.

When she entered the kitchen, Hector had just put a glass into the sink and appeared to be getting ready to leave.

"Aren't you going to eat?" she asked.

"I'll pick up a muffin or something later. I've got an early morning appointment." He scanned the length of her, then smiled. "Pretty dress."

"Thank you. Nice tie."

Silence crept between them until Hector broke it by asking, "How did you sleep?"

"Good," she lied. "How about you?"

"It took a while for me to finally doze off." He hesitated. "I worried about you, about how you were dealing with that kiss."

The fact that he'd worried about her, that he hadn't slept well, either, touched her. But she suspected that meant the kiss hadn't shaken him to the core, as it had her.

"I'm doing okay," she told him. "The kiss was nice. Maybe too nice. It left me a little unbalanced, though. It's been a long time since I was kissed like that, and I hadn't realized how much I'd missed it."

Hector sobered, and the corner of his left eye twitched—or maybe she'd just imagined it.

"I hadn't meant to remind you of Peter," he said.

"You *didn't*." Her late husband had been the last thing on her mind when they'd kissed. She could admit that much. Couldn't she? "For the record, I wasn't thinking about Peter last night."

"I'm glad to hear it." His expression lightened.

"I admit that I'm a little ruffled by whatever's going on between us, but it's only because of the babies. I realize that getting romantically involved with me would be a big step for you. And having triplets is going to make a huge change in my life, one I can hardly imagine. So there's a lot to ponder and a good reason to take things slowly. Or even to not take them at all. I'm okay with that, too."

But she wouldn't be okay, she realized. And she wondered if it might be better, safer, for her to put some distance between them.

"I feel the same way, Sam." There was the nickname again, indicating that their relationship had already taken an intimate turn, that they might never be the same two people again when this was all said and done. "Why don't we take one day at a time and see what happens?"

In that case, maybe being in close contact wasn't so bad after all.

Relief breezed through her, and she offered him a smile. "That sounds like a good game plan to me."

He reached for his sports jacket, which hung on the back of one of the kitchen chairs, and slipped it on. "So, what do you have planned today?"

More relief. She appreciated him changing the subject and switching the focus of the conversation. She answered by saying, "The wallpaper hanger is coming this morning, so I'm eager to see what the nursery looks like when he's done."

"You'd shouldn't go inside yet."

"I won't. But I'm going to talk to the painter and ask when he'll be finished."

"I imagine you're eager to move back into the house and get settled."

Actually? She was eager to set up the nursery and to finish nesting, but she wasn't looking forward to being alone again, to being sequestered in silence. She'd had enough of that in the last six months.

"I really appreciate you letting me stay here," she said. "It's been fun."

"I'm not in any hurry to see you leave. You really should let that house air out before you go back in there."

"Are you sure I'm not putting you out by staying here?"

"Not at all." He straightened the knot of his tie. "I haven't eaten this good since I lived at home with my parents."

She took that as a sincere compliment and couldn't hold back a broad smile.

Then, for some crazy reason, she moved forward, crossing the room to stand before him. Without saying a word, she reached for the knot of his tie, adjusting it even though it wasn't the least bit crooked. Then she brushed her hands across the front shoulders of his jacket, as though fixing something that was amiss.

It wasn't, though; he'd looked sharp already. She'd just wanted a chance to touch him before he left.

And to give him an opportunity to kiss her again.

When he tilted her chin with the crook of his finger, her lips parted, ready, waiting. And as he kissed her sweetly, deeply, she nearly melted into a puddle on the floor.

Earlier she'd told herself that she might be falling in love with Hector. But with each yearning beat of her heart, she realized there wasn't any doubt.

An hour after Hector left, Samantha checked in with the painter and the wallpaper hanger. Both men assured her that their work would be finished by the end of the day.

She returned to Hector's house, happy that everything was coming together nicely. Of course, there was still a lot to do, a lot to buy. But before she could focus on the nursery, she had to tell the Keatings they were going to be grandparents.

It would only take one look at her for them to see that

she was pregnant, and while she didn't mind surprising them with the news, she couldn't hold off on telling them any longer.

She'd been invited to have dinner with them next Sunday, but she still wasn't sure if it would just be the three of them. And if not, it would be cruel to spring it upon them in that way.

So instead of waiting until Sunday and arriving early, she gave Marian a call to see if she could stop by their house sometime today. It seemed to be a safer plan, all things considered.

"Of course, you can," Marian said. "But you're still planning to come over for dinner next Sunday, aren't you?"

"Yes, I am."

"Good. We've included the Hansons, too. They're practically family. You remember Don and Gloria, don't you?"

"Yes, I do." The Hansons were probably the Keatings' closest friends, but Samantha didn't want to reveal her secret in a group setting. "There's something I need to discuss with you and Randall privately, so that's why I want to stop by this morning."

"All right, we'll be waiting for you. When do you plan to come?"

Samantha glanced at the clock on Hector's mantel. "Would forty-five minutes work for you?"

"Yes, we'll see you then."

They said goodbye, and Samantha disconnected the line. After refreshing her lipstick and running a brush through her hair, she locked Hector's house and climbed into her car.

Just before ten, she gave her name to the guard at the gate of Brockman Hills, the exclusive enclave where the Keatings lived. When she was allowed in, she drove to the sprawling estate that was a far cry from the humble brownstone in which Samantha's mother had lived.

Before Samantha and Peter's wedding, Marian and Randall had tried their best to convince the couple to purchase a place in Brockman Hills, but Samantha had refused to live that close to Peter's parents. She'd feared there would be too much interference, since his parents weren't anywhere as easygoing as Peter had been. So she'd talked Peter into purchasing the house on Primrose Lane instead, which was still impressive by most people's standards.

Marian, of course, had disagreed, but that was no surprise. She'd often found Samantha's taste to be lacking.

But maybe that would change, once Marian realized that Samantha was offering them something no one else ever could.

After shutting off the ignition, Samantha took a minute to breathe deeply, to consider the words she would say. She wasn't so worried about how Randall would react, but Marian had always been...well, Marian.

Thoughts of Peter's mother reminded Samantha of the day she'd been forced to make the most difficult decision she'd ever had to make: to remove life support and let Peter die.

Marian hadn't been ready to let go of her only child, and she'd turned on Samantha as if she'd done something horrid.

"No!" Marian Keating had cried. "You *can't* do that,

Samantha. Not yet. Miracles happen every day. We'll call in the top neurologists in the country."

Randall had slipped an arm around his wife's shoulders and dropped his graying head in acceptance. "The accident has left our boy brain-dead, dear. And as much as I hate to say this, Samantha has made the right decision. We can't hang on to his body when he's already gone."

Samantha had appreciated her father-in-law's support and had clung to his words when she'd given doctors the final okay.

Randall had also acknowledged Peter's desire to be an organ donor and again nodded when Samantha had agreed to that, too.

Maybe, just maybe, when she offered the Keatings the ultimate gift of grandchildren, Marian would finally accept her and consider her a permanent part of the family.

As Samantha made her way along the walkway to the front door, she swallowed her nervousness.

Randall and Marian hadn't known about the sperm extraction, let alone the in vitro fertilization. She'd kept her secret, waiting to make sure that the implantation would take, that the pregnancy would proceed normally, that the baby—or rather babies—would be healthy.

However, after more than four months of silence, she could tell the world, starting with the Keatings. But for some reason, she was hesitant to ring the bell.

After the initial surprise, she had a feeling they'd be happy. At least, she hoped they would be.

She took a deep breath, then pushed the button. Moments later, Antonia, the Keatings' longtime house-keeper, answered the door.

Antonia smiled warmly. "Hello, Mrs. Keating." When her gaze lit upon Samantha's baby bump, she sobered, yet she held her tongue and shielded her expression. "I'll let Mrs. Keating know you're here."

"Thank you."

It had always bothered Samantha that the efficient woman had shared the same house with the Keatings, yet had never forgotten her place. Still, Samantha had always played the game whenever she came to visit, too; it had been easier that way.

As Marian entered the marble-tiled foyer, with her silver-laced hair swept into an elegant twist, she smiled—until her gaze dropped to Samantha's stomach. At that, she drew up short, and she placed a bejeweled hand upon her chest. "Oh, dear."

Randall joined her, his jovial smile fading quickly.

It had taken Peter's parents, especially his mother, a long time to warm up to her. Samantha had always believed it was because she'd grown up poor and had been a fish out of water when it came to the Keatings' social standing. But Peter had showed her the ropes, and she'd eventually caught on. But right this minute, she suspected that any headway she'd made with Peter's help had been lost.

"You remarried?" Marian asked, nearly choking on her words.

"No," Samantha said, her hand immediately shielding the mound where the babies grew. "But I have something to tell you that I hope will please you."

Marian stiffened. "I'm afraid your pregnancy is only a sad reminder that Peter wasn't able to have a family."

"That's not entirely true." Samantha pointed to the arched doorway that led to the living room. "Let's sit down. You're going to want to hear this. I promise."

Marian stood rock still for a moment. Then she began to move stiffly into the living room. Randall waited for Samantha to follow, then brought up the rear.

Once they were seated, Samantha spoke. "Five years ago, right before Peter died, we discussed having a baby."

Marian's eyes glistened, and her bottom lip quivered. But she remained stoical.

"When he was on life support, and they were—" she hated to say "harvesting his organs," which seemed so harsh, so clinical, and corrected herself in midsentence "—when they were making preparations to save the lives of others, I asked them to extract his sperm. I thought that, after time, I might like to have the baby we'd planned to have. Not right away, of course."

She'd known better than to conceive a child until after her grief passed, but it had helped during that first lonely year to know that one day a part of Peter would live on. Having Peter's son or daughter was the least she could do for the man who'd loved her and had offered her a life of luxury, as well as a peaceful, loving home.

Randall cocked his head to one side. "Are you telling me that you're pregnant with Peter's child?"

Samantha nodded, but before she could explain further, Marian asked, "Why did you wait so long to tell us?"

"At first I didn't know if the in vitro fertilization

would take. And then I wanted to make sure I got through the first trimester, since I knew how disappointed you—well, all of us—would be if something went wrong. But everything is going well."

Marian wrinkled her brow, creating a deep V in her forehead. "But you're so far along. I can't believe you waited so long to tell us. When is the baby due?"

"Not for another eighteen weeks or so."

"Eighteen more weeks?" Marian looked at Samantha's midsection and scrunched her face. "Are you sure there hasn't been some mistake?"

"Relax, Marian." Randall got to his feet. "This is a miracle we'd never anticipated. And I, for one, am thrilled to hear it."

Samantha smiled. "Actually, Randall, it's three times a miracle. I'm going to have triplets, two boys and a girl."

Marian, who usually had something to say about everything, appeared to be speechless, but in a heartfelt way.

"I would never have guessed that you might do something like this," Randall said.

"At the time, I was so heartbroken, that it was hard to think clearly. So I can't explain why I did it in the first place. I didn't want to let Peter go. And while it helped to know that through his death and the gift of his organs a lot of other people were able to live, I wasn't going to be a part of those lives. So his sperm and our dream of having a family were the only things that I was able to keep."

"This is…such a stunning surprise," Marian finally said, tears welling in her eyes. "A magical, wonderful surprise."

Samantha reached for her purse. "Would you like to see a picture of the babies?"

Marian wrinkled her brow. "Excuse me?"

Samantha pulled out the ultrasound photos that Dr. Demetrios had given her last Wednesday. She handed them to the Keatings, who immediately scooted together on the sofa so they could see their grandchildren.

"Baby A is a boy," she said. "I'm going to call him Andrew for the time being. Referring to them as letters of the alphabet sounds so cold and clinical. I've been calling Baby B Brandon and Baby C Chloe, but that will probably change as the weeks go by. I know it sounds weird, but it helps me keep them straight in my mind when the doctor talks about them and their positions."

"I would think you'd want to name the first-born boy Peter Randall Keating," Marian said. "It would mean a lot to us."

Samantha supposed it would. But she'd already gone above and beyond for the Keatings. If things continued to develop between her and Hector, she didn't feel comfortable naming one of the babies after Peter. It just didn't seem right.

And even if Hector weren't involved in her life, she didn't want to single out one boy over the other, even when it came to a name. So she decided to speak her mind, hopefully putting an end to any further discussion about it. "If there was only one boy, I might have considered that, Marian. But I don't want there to be any jealousy or hard feelings between them, so I'll give them their own names."

Randall and Marian grew quiet for a moment, their eyes focused on the grainy ultrasound photos.

Samantha wondered if they would argue or object to her reason for not naming either boy Peter, but they didn't.

When Randall finally looked up, his eyes red-rimmed and swimming in emotion, he said, "You have no idea how much this means to us, Samantha."

Marian opened her mouth to speak, then choked on the words, as tears slid down her cheeks, smearing her mascara. She finally sniffled and said, "I can't believe it." She reached for her husband's hand, gave it an affectionate squeeze and peered at him with watery eyes. "We're going to be grandparents after all, honey. I can't wait to tell our friends."

Randall offered her a loving grin, then turned to Samantha. "Is there anything you need? Anything at all?"

"No. I'm fine. Peter took very good care of me, even after he passed away."

And he had. He'd kept his trust in order, and everything that had been his was now hers.

"You must have loved him dearly," Marian said. "I knew that you did, but to do this for him…for us…"

"Peter was a wonderful man, and we lost him too soon." Samantha had loved him, of course. How could she not have? And she would never forget him. But she'd moved on in her life and looked forward to creating a family of her own.

A family she'd be sharing with the Keatings.

She wondered how Hector would feel about that.

* * *

On Saturday morning, Hector went to Samantha's house and opened up the windows to air it out. The work was finished, and the only sign that the painter had been there was the lingering paint fumes.

After the house had been aired out for an hour or more, Hector agreed to let Samantha take a quick look at the nursery before he would usher her back outside again.

"It's darling," she said. "I'm so happy I chose that wallpaper pattern. I can't wait to hang white eyelet curtains and to fill the room with furniture. In fact, I think I'll go shopping and buy the cribs today."

"I could drive you," he said. "If you want me to."

"Really?" she asked, those blue eyes sparking with her smile.

Well, it wasn't exactly his first choice of things to do on a Saturday, like the golf game he'd canceled. But he'd come to enjoy her company, and she'd be going back home soon.

"Sure," he told her. "I don't have anything better to do."

Fifteen minutes later, they parked at The Baby Boutique and went inside.

Hector was amazed at all the odds and ends that filled the store. Who would have guessed babies needed so much stuff?

They went right to the furniture section, where he looked for the white crib she'd seen in the newspaper ad. He spotted it near a display of teddy bears and pointed it out.

"What do you think?" she asked as she ran a hand along the railing.

He thought it appeared to be a functional baby bed, but something told him she was looking for a better response than that. "It ought to look good in the nursery, although it might get cramped in there with three cribs."

"I'll probably only buy one dresser, so I think it will all fit."

As she checked out the mattress, he scanned the shelves of stuffed animals, grabbing three bears—one brown, the others white and black. "This will be my contribution to the nursery."

She spotted the stuffed teddy bears in his arms and smiled. "You don't have to do that, Hector."

"I want to."

"Then thank you." She continued to study him, her eyes filled with some kind of emotion he didn't dare question, emotion that seemed to have a lot more value than the cost of three little bears.

When they were interrupted by a salesclerk, a matronly brunette, Samantha ordered three cribs and a matching dresser. She also picked out mattresses that were the top of the line.

"It'll take about a week to ten days for these to come in," the clerk said.

"Can I have them delivered?"

"You bet." The clerk wrote up the order then asked for Samantha's address.

She paid for the furniture with her credit card, and Hector whipped out a couple of twenties for the stuffed bears. Instead of waiting for the clerk to go to another station to find a big enough bag, they walked toward the store exit with his purchase in his arms.

"How about an ice-cream cone?" Hector asked. "There's a shop not far from here that offers a huge selection."

Samantha cast him a pretty smile. "Here you are, carrying three stuffed animals and asking for an ice-cream cone. How cute is that?"

It was probably more sappy than cute, he supposed, but he didn't care. He was looking forward to seeing that nursery come together, too.

They were both grinning from ear to ear when they walked out of the store. Before they could head toward the parking lot, a familiar voice rang out. "Hey, would you look at that."

Hector turned to see Yolanda, who was carrying a shopping bag that was stuffed to the brim.

Yolanda glanced at the teddy bears in Hector's arms and laughed. "You stopped here to buy stuffed animals?"

"Actually," Samantha said, "I ordered the furniture for the nursery. It's going to be delivered next week."

"What's in the bag?" Hector asked his sister.

"Things I want to return. My friends threw a baby shower for me last Saturday, and I got way too many of some things and not enough of others." Yolanda turned to Samantha. "Have you had a shower yet?"

"No, not yet. I'm really not expecting one, though. But that's okay. I'm having fun buying things. And on the bright side, that means I won't have anything to exchange."

Yolanda shuffled her bag from one hand to the other. "Everyone needs to have a shower. Besides, with a first baby, there's so much you need to get. And you're going to need three times as much. Without a shower, it'll be expensive."

Hector didn't see any point in telling his sister that Samantha didn't have any financial worries.

"Well," he said, "I'd like to get these teddy bears into the car before someone I know spots me with them."

Yolanda laughed. "I'm someone you know."

"You don't count," Hector said.

"Maybe not, but I sure wish I had a camera so I could show Mom. She'd love to see a picture of my macho brother getting soft around the edges."

"Mom doesn't count, either, although I'd hate to have those pictures get out. I was more concerned about one of the other attorneys in my firm or maybe opposing counsel seeing me with my arms full of stuffed animals."

"It's amazing what the arrival of little babies will do to us, isn't it?"

His sister had a point, he realized, although it wasn't the babies but their mama that was doing that to him. He was definitely softening, though. He'd be golfing today if he hadn't decided to hang out with Samantha instead.

"I won't keep you," Yolanda said, "but I'd like you to come to my house next Saturday afternoon around four."

"What's going on?" Hector asked.

She paused, as though thinking of a response, then said. "Chad and I are having a combination potluck/taco bar. For the most part, it'll be very casual. And it will just be family."

"It's okay with me." Hector glanced at Samantha, who shrugged and said, "I don't have any plans."

"Then Saturday it is," Yolanda said with a smile.

Hector could see the wheels in her mind turning. Was she making assumptions about his love life again? Or was she planning something other than tacos next Saturday? He wasn't sure, but he'd give her a call later to find out.

He didn't mind surprises, as long as he was springing them on someone else.

"I'd better go," Yolanda said, her eyes lighting up in a way that suggested she really was up to something. "I've got a lot to do, and not much time to do it."

So she did have something up her sleeve. Knowing his sister, it could be anything. But he kept his thoughts to himself as he and Samantha started toward the parking space where he'd left his car.

He glanced at the teddy bears he held. He wished he'd waited for the salesclerk to get the shopping bag.

If his arms weren't full, he would have slipped his hand in hers.

Chapter Eleven

Samantha officially moved back to her house on Monday morning, but she and Hector continued to eat dinner together each night.

During the day, while she nested, he would call her from the office every now and then. Sometimes he'd ask if she wanted him to pick up anything on his way home, while at others he just wanted to check on her and see if she was all right.

It didn't matter what she was doing when the phone rang, whenever she heard his voice on the line, it brought a smile to her heart, as well as her lips.

They'd kissed several times, each one more arousing than the next, but they hadn't made love. They'd broached the subject last night, though, after a kiss that had left them both breathless.

"There's nothing I'd like more," Hector had said as he rose up on an elbow while lying next to her on his bed. "But I don't feel comfortable making love until after you run it by your doctor. I know he's keeping close tabs on you."

"I'll call him in the morning. Maybe he'll give us the okay."

He'd smiled, then brushed a strand of hair from her face. "And if he doesn't, it'll be okay. We'll wait until it is."

It was then that she realized the depths of her love for him. And she hoped that he felt the same about her. Either way, they'd become more than neighbors, more than friends. They'd become a couple.

The next morning, she'd called Dr. Demetrios's office and asked to speak to him.

"He's not in today," Sara Beth, the head nurse, said. "But he'll be back on Monday. Is this an emergency?"

Samantha's libido insisted that it most definitely was, but she said, "No. I'll wait until he's back in the office."

She hung up the phone, then fixed the pot roast for dinner.

After they'd eaten, Hector and Samantha sat on the sofa in his family room and watched a movie, a cozy, nightly habit they'd both come to enjoy.

It was interesting, though. She might spend the days at her own house, but at night, it went without saying that they would hang out at Hector's.

She wasn't sure why that was. She'd thought about it, though. And while neither of them had brought up the subject, she wondered if they chose his house because it had been home to them during the time hers was being painted and she'd stayed with him.

There was one other possibility, one she hated to admit: Peter's ghost wasn't there.

Not that her house was haunted or anything. It was just that, earlier today, while she'd been dusting the furniture in the living room, she'd noticed a piece of artwork Peter had liked, as well as the easy chair on which he'd preferred to read, and she'd realized that a part of him had remained behind.

She'd made up her mind to buy new furniture and to redecorate as soon as she could. She wasn't actually trying to exorcise his memory or essence from the house, but if she and Hector were going to build a life together—assuming that's the direction their relationship was heading—it wouldn't help if everywhere Hector turned he saw Peter's wife, his children and his personal belongings.

They could only avoid her house for so long, though. Once the triplets arrived, they would have to spend more time in the house with the nursery.

So Samantha had called Helen Gilmore, the director of the battered women's shelter, and donated her furniture for use at the safe houses or the apartments that provided transitional living.

Helen had been thrilled at the offer and had promised to send a truck for everything early next week. And when Samantha had ended the call, she'd felt good about what she'd done. Once she'd brought in a decorator and purchased new furniture, she could make the house her own.

As she watched the movie, Hector's arm slipped around her shoulders. She leaned into him, and the side of her leg pressed against his. She splayed her left hand on top of his thigh and the other on her ever-expanding belly.

When a definite flutter moved in her tummy, her breath caught.

Hector immediately tensed and turned to face her. "What's the matter, Sam?"

"I think one of the babies moved."

"Really?" A look of awe washed away one of concern. "Can I feel it?"

"You can try." She reached for his hand, placed it where hers had been, where she'd felt the little one move. "I'd been having these bubblelike flutters and didn't know what it was. But this time, it was much stronger. And I knew it had to be one of the babies."

They waited, joined in wonder, but as one minute stretched into the next, it didn't appear as though the baby was going to cooperate.

"I'm sorry," she finally said. "Whoever was turning somersaults must have decided to take a nap."

"Maybe next time," he said, his voice laced with a hint of disappointment.

Before either of them could settle back in their cozy seats and focus on the movie, Samantha's cell phone rang. She had no idea who could be calling her, although she hoped it was someone from The Baby Boutique, telling her the cribs and dresser had come in and wanting to schedule the delivery.

So she got to her feet, feeling as graceful as a duck in high heels, and practically waddled across the room to the table on which she'd left her purse.

"Hello?"

"Hi, dear. I hope I didn't disturb you."

It was Marian, Samantha realized. And her voice was more cheerful than usual.

"It's no bother. I was just watching TV with a friend." She glanced at Hector, saw him watching her.

Okay, so they were more than friends.

She'd have to tell Marian about Hector one of these days, but what was there to tell when neither of them had any idea where their relationship would end up or how long it might last? Not that she wasn't entertaining thoughts of marriage.

If and when things became more serious, she'd have to tell Randall and Marian about the man she'd fallen in love with, the man she hoped would be a father to Peter's children.

Her stomach knotted at the thought, at their reaction. But like Hector suggested, she would take one day at a time.

"I won't keep you," Marian said. "But Gloria Hanson would like to host a baby-shower luncheon for you at the country club. It'll be a lovely affair, but she'll need to book the garden room. So we wanted to know what days you're available."

"It's a little early, isn't it?"

"Well, since triplets don't always go to term, and since you might even end up on bed rest down the road, we thought it would be best to schedule it sooner rather than later."

"I'm not home right now, so I can't check my calendar. Can I get back to you on that?"

"Of course," Marian said. "By the way, Randall and I would love to go shopping with you for the cribs and the bedding. We're so excited, we can hardly stand it."

Samantha glanced over her shoulder and peered at Hector, who was watching her rather than the television. She didn't want to shortchange the Keatings, she'd already purchased the big items—with Hector. And if truth be told, she'd prefer to have Hector as a shopping companion, if he was willing to go with her again.

But now wasn't the time to discuss any of that.

"Why don't I give you a call tomorrow morning?" she suggested.

"All right, I'll talk to you then. Good night, dear. And have fun with your friend."

"Thanks." She wondered how Marian would feel when she learned that the friend in question was male.

When she hung up the phone and headed back toward the sofa, Hector asked, "Who was that?"

Samantha had always valued honesty, even though she hadn't come out and told Hector that the babies were going to be Keatings yet. "It was Peter's mother."

"What did *she* want?" His tone came across crisp and tight, as if he wasn't happy about the call or the fact Samantha and Marian still had a connection.

But she was more connected to the Keatings now than ever.

"I'm going to their house for dinner on Sunday, and she mentioned lunch at the country club one of these days."

Hector studied her momentarily, then returned to watching the movie.

Was he bothered by Marian's invitation?

Or had he forgotten the phone call already?

Maybe she was reading way too much into his question, his silence.

Still, she couldn't help but wonder what would become of their relationship—or whatever it was—when he found out *all* the details about the in vitro.

He shouldn't mind. After all, he'd assumed that she'd used a stranger as a sperm donor. And in this case, she knew exactly who the father really was. So there was no reason to question the genetics.

As she settled in beside him on the sofa, the secret stretched taut between them, and she wondered if she should bite the bullet and tell him now.

Maybe, but if she waited until she'd redecorated the living room and bought new bedding and curtains for the bedroom, she could show him that Peter was no longer a part of her life, of her heart.

It wouldn't take long to give her house a fresh, new look.

And then she'd tell him.

While Hector played golf with his buddies on Saturday, Samantha met with a decorator and hired her to give the interior of the house an entirely new look. Then she made a list of all the things she wanted to donate to the women's shelter.

When she was finished, she felt an inexplicable sense of relief, although not because she'd wiped out all signs of Peter in the house. She'd kept some of his personal items to pass on to the babies when they grew up, such as his watch, his favorite books and his journals. But when she moved back into the house after five years away, she'd experienced an eerie feeling, as if she'd stepped into a time warp.

With Peter's presence still thick within the walls, she'd been constantly reminded of his loss, of her sadness, her grief, and she hadn't appreciated the reminder. Not when her future appeared brighter now than ever before.

So she patted herself on the back for having the gumption to make the necessary changes in her life, took a long, refreshing shower and got dressed to attend taco night at Yolanda's.

After fixing her hair and applying pink lipstick and a dab of mascara, she slipped into her nicest maternity dress, a black classic cut with plenty of give in the waist. She hadn't gotten used to having the baby bump so pronounced, especially when it seemed to be growing bigger with each passing hour, but it was the style.

She gave herself a once-over in the mirror before returning to Hector's house shortly before he got home from the golf course.

When he entered the house, he held a shopping bag in his arms. But before she could quiz him about what was inside, his face lit up, and he said, "Wow. You look great, Sam."

She placed her hand on her belly. "Are you sure? I feel a little self-conscious."

"You shouldn't." He closed the distance between them and pressed a kiss on her forehead. "You're the prettiest expectant mother I've ever known."

His words touched her nearly as much as his kiss.

"Give me a few minutes to shower," he said, "and then we can go to Yolanda's."

"All right." Her gaze was drawn to his shopping bag. "But what have you got in there?"

"Something for the babies." He reached inside and pulled out a blue corduroy pickup truck that had been stitched and stuffed.

He tossed it to her, and she caught it. Then she watched him withdraw a matching tractor, which had been made by the same manufacturer. He transferred it to the crook of his arm while he removed a stuffed doll made out of soft flannel. "And this is for Chloe. What do you think? Should I have gotten her a car, too? They had a fire truck that was kind of cool."

Happy tears filled her eyes, and emotion balled in her throat. "The doll is just fine. Thank you, Hector."

His head cocked slightly, and he furrowed his brow. "Is something wrong?"

"No, I'm just touched by your thoughtfulness, that's all."

"It's not a big deal."

But it was a very big deal to her. Hector had been thinking about the babies today, and he'd gone out of his way to do something for them. And that made her think that when they were born, the five of them might become a family someday. Before this moment, she hadn't realized just how badly she'd like that to happen.

Besides, even though he hadn't actually fathered the babies, he appeared to be bonding with them. At least, he was certainly giving it an all-out try.

As Hector glanced down at the tractor and grinned, she spotted a glimpse of the little boy he'd once been. She wondered what a child of theirs might look like, but she shook off the sentiment and tried to focus on the here and now.

"We're supposed to be at your sister's house at five-thirty," she said. "So you'd better get in the shower."

"Okay." He handed her the stuffed toys he'd been holding. "I'll be back in a flash."

Twenty minutes later, Samantha sat in the passenger seat of Hector's car as they headed to Yolanda and Chad's house.

She was a little nervous about attending the taco fest and meeting the rest of Hector's family, but she'd hit it off almost immediately with his sister, so she'd told herself everything was going to be fine.

As Hector turned down a tree-lined street, she peered out the passenger window and spotted children playing on the grass in several front yards. "This looks like a nice neighborhood."

"It is." Hector pulled along the curb in the cul-de-sac and parked in front of a pale yellow house with redbrick trim. "I think it's going to be great place for my sister and Chad to raise a family."

He got out of the car, but Samantha climbed out without waiting for him to get her door.

Still, as they made their way along the sidewalk and toward the house, Hector reached for her hand and gave it a warm and fortifying squeeze.

It felt good to be a couple, and the physical connection chased away her nervousness.

As they stood before a heart-shaped welcome mat, Hector rang the bell.

Moments later, Yolanda hollered, "Come on in."

Hector opened the door, then waited for Samantha to enter first. As she stepped into the hardwood entryway, a chorus of voices yelled, "Surprise!"

It took her a moment to realize that the surprise was on her. And that Yolanda's house had been decorated for a baby shower with streamers and posters of storks and baby bottles and rattles.

All she could say was, "I don't understand…?"

"Every pregnant woman deserves a baby shower," Yolanda said.

As Hector's sister reached out to give Samantha a welcoming hug, their bellies got in the way, and they had to duck and twist. They chuckled at the awkwardness, and so did the others.

"I don't know what to say." Samantha had never been so taken aback—or so honored—in all her life.

"It's just a small party," Yolanda said as she led Samantha and Hector into the living room, where smiling faces greeted her. "Mostly family. But I wanted to make sure you had a shower of some kind."

"Mom and Dad," Yolanda said, as she led Samantha toward a middle-aged couple she introduced as Jorge and Carmen. "This is our guest of honor."

Samantha reached out her hand in greeting, first to Hector's mother, a petite woman in her late-fifties. And then to his father, a tall man with silver-laced dark hair. "I'm pleased to meet you."

Next she met Hector's younger brother, Diego, a

handsome man in his late twenties. His wife, Alicia, was a hairdresser.

There were two other couples, friends of the family she was told. And when she'd met everyone, she was led to the dining room, where the food had been spread upon a long table like a buffet. Fried tortilla shells, spiced chicken and beef, lettuce, tomatoes and grated cheese had been set out in brightly colored dishes. There were also bowls of guacamole, salsa and sour cream available.

"So this is a taco fest." Samantha smiled up at Hector. "It looks good."

"Chad," Yolanda said from the doorway as she made her way into the room wearing a pair of oven mitts and carrying a casserole dish. "I need you to make some room for Mama's chicken mole. And then you'll need to bring in the beans and rice."

"Didn't I tell you that my sister was bossy?" Hector said with a spark of affection in his tone. "I swear, poor Chad should be sainted."

In her own defense, a smiling Yolanda said to Samantha, "If the men in my life didn't need a bit of a push every now and then, I wouldn't have to crack the whip."

Moments later, Yolanda told everyone to fill their plates, and before long, they'd eaten their fill.

"Everything was delicious," Samantha told Hector's sister.

"Thanks," Yolanda said. "I'm afraid I can't take all the credit. My mom made most of it, and she's the best cook in town."

"I'll have to get your recipe for chicken mole, Mrs. Garza. I've never eaten it before, but it's really tasty."

"Please, call me Carmen. And I'd be happy to give you my recipe. It's Hector's favorite dish."

Apparently, rumor was out that Hector and Samantha were more than friends, or maybe it just seemed that way. But she had to admit, the Garza family and their friends were nice people. She would look forward to joining one of their get-togethers anytime.

"It's time to open your presents," Yolanda said as she ushered Samantha to a rocking chair near a small table laden with gifts.

The rocker, she realized, was the heirloom that Hector had told her about. And as she took a seat, she felt privileged to be a part of the family—if just for today.

She received mostly clothing—preemie outfits from Yolanda, who said she'd heard triplets tended to be smaller at birth. And baby bottles, pacifiers, rattles.

When she hadn't been looking, Hector had disappeared, and, when he returned, he carried a white cradle with a bright red bow. "There are two more of these hidden in my garage at home."

"It's beautiful," she said, "and it matches the cribs."

"I had my secretary call around, then drive all over town to buy three that matched so we wouldn't have to order them."

"You'll have to thank her for me."

He grinned. "Are you kidding? She was thrilled to do it. Apparently, no one has ever paid her to go shopping before, and she wondered if I needed anything from Nordstrom."

Samantha laughed, then turned to everyone in the room. "Thank you so much for thinking of me and the babies. You have no idea how much this means or how much I appreciate it. I'll never forget your kindness."

Then she got up from the chair and gave Yolanda a hug. Well, she tried to. They had the same problem with their pregnant bellies getting in the way.

"Let's get some pictures of you by the cake," Yolanda said.

Moments later, as flashes from several cameras went off, Samantha couldn't help but smile. She was going to have a ton of pictures, which was great. She wanted something to help her remember this day and how special it had been.

The Garzas were wonderful people, and she was so glad that she had the chance to meet them. She couldn't help comparing them to the Keatings. The couples were so different from one another, yet she realized her children would benefit from knowing both families.

"Hey," Yolanda said to Hector as she reached for a knife to cut the cake. "Why don't you take Samantha into the living room and get cozy?"

Hector, who'd been watching the amateur photo shoot with a grin, said, "I'd be happy to."

He placed a hand on Samantha's lower back and guided her out of the small dining room and into the living room.

"Surprised?" he asked.

"You have no idea."

"I knew Yolanda was up to something, and she called a couple of days ago to give me a heads-up. I hope you don't mind that I kept it a secret."

"That's fine."

Hector was tempted to reach for her hand, to hold it as he had so many times when they'd been home alone, but he wasn't quite sure he ought to make a public display in front of his family. He didn't need them to press him for more details than he was willing to share. At least, not until he knew for sure where their relationship was heading.

He had a pretty good idea, though. He was getting dangerously close to falling for Samantha, if he hadn't done so already.

As they sat side by side, he stole a glance at her, saw her hand resting on her belly.

Last night, as he'd leaned close and waited for one of the babies to move, he hadn't felt anything. But he'd smelled Samantha's springtime-scent, felt the warmth of her breath and the throb of her pulse just under the skin, and he'd been hard-pressed not to carry her to his bed.

But he would bide his time until her doctor gave the okay. There was no way he'd put her at risk for premature labor and jeopardize the health of the babies.

Damn. He was more attracted to Samantha than he'd been to another woman in years.

Or ever.

He snuck another glance her way. Would she think he was out of line if he reached over and touched her belly again?

Yolanda had let him feel her baby tumbling around once, and it had been amazing. But he didn't think this was the place to ask.

They stayed and visited for another half hour or so, and as everyone began to leave, Hector leaned toward Samantha and whispered, "Are you ready to go, too?"

"Sure. Do you mind if I use the bathroom first?"

"Not at all." He got to his feet, then reached out to help her up. He held her hand, as well as her gaze, for a bit longer than necessary. Then he watched her leave the room.

He must have had a wistful stare on his face, because his mother eased close to him and said, "She's a lovely woman, *mijo*."

"I know."

"Is it serious?"

What should he tell her? Yes, it is? No, not yet? But his mother had always been able to see right through him, even when others couldn't. "It seems to be getting that way."

"For what it's worth, your father and I like her. And we've noticed a glow about you."

Hoping to diffuse the seriousness of the conversation, he laughed it off. "Don't tell me that pregnant glows are contagious."

"Don't make light of it, *mijo*. For the past few years, whenever you walked into a family party or get-together, there was always a cloud of tension hanging over you. But it's gone, and an aura of happiness surrounds you now. So don't blame me for wanting it to last."

He didn't respond, didn't dare to.

When Samantha returned, they said goodbye and climbed into his car. On the way home, she told him how much she enjoyed being with his family, how much she liked his sister.

"Diego's nice, too," she said. "Chad told me that he just got his contractor's license and has started his own company."

"That's true. He's always worked in construction, so I'm glad to see him take that step. In fact, he's the one who suggested I buy the house on Primrose Lane. He'd heard it was a distress sale and knew I'd been looking for a good deal on a fixer in a nice neighborhood. It was pretty run-down and needed work, but the price was right. And Diego did most of the work for me."

"It must be nice to have loving siblings who look out for you. My babies are going to be lucky that way."

Hector suspected her kids were going to be fortunate, but mostly because they would have a great mother.

Five minutes later, Hector turned onto Primrose Lane and drove to his house, figuring he'd just park in his driveway and carry Samantha's baby gifts to her house.

Maybe, afterward, they'd put on a movie.

But as he neared his place, he spotted a cream-colored Bentley parked in front of Samantha's house.

"Looks like you've got company," he said.

"It's Randall and Marian Keating."

He'd never met the couple, but annoyance settled over him, and he wondered why they had to show up and put a damper on what otherwise had been a nice evening.

Chapter Twelve

Hector pulled into his driveway and parked, but his movements were stiff as he swung open the door and climbed out of the Beemer.

It shouldn't bother him that Peter's parents had stopped by to see Samantha. And it shouldn't surprise him that they'd maintained a connection. After all, Mrs. Keating had called Samantha the other day and had invited her to the house for dinner—and to the country club for lunch in the future.

But even that phone call had made him uneasy.

Before he could open the passenger door for Samantha, she'd done so herself. Then she strode toward the ultra-luxury sedan that must have cost well over a hundred grand, maybe even two.

Noting her approach, the well-dressed couple in their mid-sixties exited their car and met her partway.

"I guess we should have called first," Mrs. Keating said, as she greeted Samantha with a hug and one of those air-smacking kisses.

A part of Hector wanted to be polite and retreat into his house so Samantha and her former in-laws could talk alone, yet another, more territorial and vocal part of him insisted that he greet the Keatings, too. That he let them know he was involved with her, at least on some level.

Needless to say, the side of him that harbored his better judgment lost. So he sauntered toward the couple and slapped an easy-going grin on his face when he felt anything but.

When Mrs. Keating looked up and noticed him, her perfectly coifed head tilted slightly, her eyes narrowed and her expression clouded.

"This is my neighbor," Samantha said. "Hector Garza."

The use of the word *neighbor* to describe him stung like jalapeño juice on a paper cut, and he prickled. But he reached out a hand in greeting, first to Peter's father, then to his mother.

"How do you do?" Randall said.

"Great."

Returning his focus to Samantha, the older man said, "We stopped by to see how you're doing."

Marian added, "And to ask if we could see what you've done with the nursery so far, to see what you might need."

They certainly seemed supportive of their former

daughter-in-law and her new family; he'd have to give them credit for that.

"If you need anything," Randall said, "anything at all, just let us know. We still can't believe you'd do this for us."

Do *what* for them?

Hector's mind sparked, just as it did when he was on the verge of catching a witness in a bald-faced lie on the stand.

Samantha splayed her hand over her belly, as though shielding her babies. He stole a peek at her face, only to see that she'd paled, that she wore a pregnant-doe-in-the-headlights expression. At least, it seemed to him that she had.

Damn, Hector thought. What in the hell had she done? Had she offered them a grandparent role in her babies' lives?

If so, he wasn't sure how he felt about that.

"Oh, dear," Marian said. "Randall, I can't believe I left that photo album in the car. Will you get it for me, sweetheart?"

Randall chuckled. "She had poor Antonia looking high and low for that thing. She wanted to show you pictures of Peter as a baby. She thought you might enjoy seeing what he looked like."

As Randall went out to the car, Hector drew himself up straight and tried to sort through what was being said, tried to grasp the subtext under the surface.

"With three babies," Marian said, "I'm sure one will take after its father."

Father? Peter had been the sperm donor?

Oh, for cripe's sake. The Armstrong Fertility Institute. In vitro fertilization.

What do you know about the father? he'd asked her.

Actually, quite a bit.

It didn't take a brain surgeon to connect the dots, and he felt as though someone had kicked him in the gut. And that someone was Samantha.

Why hadn't she told him?

"Hey, listen," he said to her. "I'll bring those gifts over later." He nodded toward his house. "I've got some things I need to do while you show your in-laws the nursery."

He could have thought of them as her former in-laws, but that was clearly not the case. Samantha had never gotten over Peter's death. She still loved him. How could she not? In fact, she planned to have some kind of family with the guy, just as though he'd taken a trip to Europe and would be back next month.

There were a hundred times she could have told him that she'd frozen Peter's sperm, that she'd decided to have a dead man's family. But she'd clearly held back, keeping it a secret.

Why?

It made no sense. But he knew one thing, if she'd been upfront with him, they never would have gotten involved; they never would have kissed.

"I'll talk to you later," she said. "Okay?"

"Sure." But he didn't want to hear any explanations, any excuses. He just wanted to go home and lick his wounds. But then again, with those baby gifts in the trunk of his car, he'd be forced to listen.

As he reached the front door, Randall returned with

the photo album and gave it to his wife. "On second thought," Hector said. "Randall, why don't you come with me? Samantha has some baby gifts in the trunk of my car. You can help me carry them inside her house."

There weren't that many gifts, so with Randall's help, they made fast work of the chore.

As Hector carried the cradle toward the front door, he glanced Samantha's way and caught her eye. Her gaze seemed to say *We need to talk; I can explain.* But he wasn't up for it. Not now.

After dropping the gifts and the cradle off in the nursery, Hector let himself out of her house. He'd hoped to feel some relief after he left, but even as he crossed the lawn into his own yard, his heart ached like a son of a gun.

He let himself into the house and shut the door, still hoping for that sense of relief. But there was none to be found.

Samantha's betrayal and his disappointment hurt like hell, and for some reason, the pain that lingered was far worse than it had been when Patrice had left him.

Samantha was heartsick that Hector had learned her secret the way he had, and she kicked herself for not telling him sooner.

Who would have guessed that the Keatings would just stop by unannounced like that? They'd never done so before.

If she hadn't been so unbalanced by the mess she'd made of her budding relationship, of the pain she'd seen on Hector's face and his fierce attempt to hide it, she would have thought their enthusiasm for their new grandbabies was sweet. But all she could think of was sending the couple on their way so she could walk next door and try to pick up the pieces of a romance that had scarcely gotten off the ground before it crashed and burned.

Hector had put up a false front, but she'd seen him stiffen, seen the tension in his brow. She'd wanted to explain, to tell him that she loved him, that she was sorry. But she'd had to wait for over an hour for Marian and Randall to leave.

As soon as the Bentley was out of the neighborhood, she headed to Hector's. In the past, she would have let herself in, using the key he'd given her if she had to. But something told her she needed an invitation this time.

She rang the bell, then waited for him to answer.

And then she waited some more.

Was he in the shower? Out in the garage or in the backyard? Impulsively, she reached for the knob, then drew back her hand again.

About the time she was going to turn around and head back home, the door swung open. But just partially.

"Hey," she said, trying to manage a smile.

But it didn't seem to work.

"Why didn't you tell me?" he asked.

"I didn't think it was any of your business at first. And then… Well, I wasn't sure how you'd take it."

He crossed his arms, making his biceps flex. "Were you *ever* going to tell me?"

"Of course!"

"When?" he asked. "Before or after the kids went to kindergarten?"

"I thought that—"

"That I'd never need to know? That I'd probably never find out? That wasn't fair, Sam." Anger and disappointment flared on his face, and she realized he wasn't just dragging his feet about letting her in the house this evening. He was actually shutting her out of his home, out of his life.

And she could hardly blame him. "You're right, Hector, and I'm sorry. I'd really like to work through this."

"I don't see how we can. Peter is going to be a part of your life for as long as you live."

She placed her hand on her belly, shielding the kids from the truth, which shouldn't be so painful, but it was.

"I didn't realize how much you despised him."

"It's not that I hated him. I just didn't like him very much. I didn't respect him, either. And for what it's worth, those feelings were mutual."

"And you're holding that animosity against me and three babies?"

"No, I'm not. But I'm not going to compete with a memory. The best I'd ever do is come second place." He straightened his stance, digging in his heels, it seemed. "And on top of that, a relationship based on a lie, even one of omission, doesn't stand a chance in hell."

She wanted to argue otherwise, but how could she when she realized he was right?

For a moment, she opened her mouth to tell him that she loved him, to promise that she'd never keep anything from him again. But what was the use? They had two strikes against them already: he'd already made up his mind, and the babies she was carrying were Peter's.

The third and final strike was a given: no matter how much she loved Hector, her children would have to come first.

Hector had held his ground on Saturday night like a true champ, but he hadn't felt at all like a winner. His sense of loss had been too great.

It had taken him ages to fall asleep, and he'd tossed and turned until dawn. Instead of feeling refreshed, he woke in a foul mood and ready to snap.

After breakfast, he decided to take the cradles he'd been storing in his garage to Samantha's house. He wasn't looking forward to rehashing the words they'd had yesterday or revisiting the pain of her deceit and ultimate rejection.

Still, when she failed to answer the door, and he realized she wasn't home, he'd been more disappointed than he would have imagined. But he was determined to face the facts; whatever they'd had was over.

He still had the spare key to her house that she'd given him, so he let himself in and placed the cradles in the center of the living room where she was sure to see them. Then he left her keys on the mattress of one of them.

Maybe he was taking the coward's way out by not handing over the keys personally, but if he talked to her for any length of time, he was afraid he'd roll over. And then where would he be?

Whatever they'd shared, whatever he'd hoped it might have become, had died a fool's death.

Yet that didn't make him feel the least bit better.

When Samantha had come over to apologize the other night, for a moment he'd waffled and almost said, "Sure. Why not? Let's see where this relationship is headed. I'll play second fiddle to your first husband."

But he knew where it was headed—*nowhere.*

And he'd never played back-up to anyone in his life. As far as he was concerned, second place was the same thing as first loser. So he'd stood straight and proud.

And broken.

As she'd turned to walk away, he'd watched her go, but only for a minute. It hurt too bad to stand there and suffer in silence. So he'd closed the door, hoping to shut out the sense of betrayal, the sense of pain.

Instead, he'd suffered a crushing blow that had hurt a hell of a lot more than when Patrice had left him.

It was then that he'd realized he'd fallen hopelessly in love with Samantha. But he'd also been faced with the fact that she still loved a memory, that she'd never be able to let Peter go. And that his kids would be an ever-constant reminder of the mental and emotional memorial she'd built for him in her heart.

With that being the case, then how could he ever expect to have a healthy relationship with her?

He couldn't.

Of course, realizing that still didn't make it any easier to accept.

Four days later, while he was leaving for work, he saw Samantha dragging her recycle bins out to the road.

Dammit, she shouldn't be doing that in her condition. He started to get out of his car, but stopped himself.

Did he really want to get sucked into her life again?

Did he want to compete with a memory, knowing he'd always come up short?

No, but he couldn't sit here and watch her struggle with those bins. So he shifted into Park, turned off the ignition and climbed from the car.

He'd barely circled the vehicle when he saw her slip and take a hard fall, right into the street.

Oh, no. He rushed to her side. "Sam, are you okay?"

"Ow," she cried. "I…I don't know. Everything hurts." She clutched her belly, and the fear on her face was disarming.

Hector no longer gave a rat's ass about secrets or frozen DNA or long-lost love.

What if Samantha was injured? What if the fall had hurt one of the babies? What if she'd jarred something—or someone—loose?

"I'll take you to the doctor's office," he said. "We can call once we're in the car and let them know we're on the way."

"But—"

"No buts about it, Sam." He helped her up, supported her as she winced in pain.

"What hurts, honey?"

"My ankle. I twisted it. That's what caused me to fall. I landed on my hip, and everything pretty much aches."

He walked her slowly to the car, wondering if he should have called an ambulance instead. But she was up. And walking. So he helped her into the passenger seat and adjusted the seat belt. Then he climbed behind the wheel.

Everything was pumping—his heart, his blood, his

adrenaline. Before backing out of the driveway, he called his office and asked his secretary to reschedule all of his meetings for the rest of the day. Then he pulled into the street.

"Where's the doctor's office?" he asked.

"It's located in the clinic next to the Armstrong Fertility Institute."

The silence was almost overwhelming, as words and emotion jammed in Hector's throat.

Twenty minutes later, they arrived at the obstetrician's office. Again Hector helped her out of the car and up the walkway. Once inside the clinic, Samantha was walking better, but still limping.

"How are you feeling now?" he asked.

"Okay. I'm a little shaky, though."

Hector followed her to the receptionist, a woman in her mid- to late-fifties.

The woman smiled warmly. "Hello, Mrs. Keating. I'll let Sara Beth know you're here. But don't take a seat. Go on in—they're expecting you."

Hector couldn't help noting that the receptionist didn't call Samantha by name, and he didn't like the fact that she was clinging to the Keating surname, as if it was another way of holding on to Peter.

But he didn't have time or the inclination to split hairs about that now. All he wanted to know was that she was all right and that the babies were, too.

They'd no more than reached the center of the waiting room when a red-haired nurse wearing bright pink scrubs opened the door and called, "Samantha."

Her first name, he realized, feeling a bit better.

Once they were settled in the exam room, Hector held her hand as she climbed onto the table. Then he took a seat in the chair next to the window. They didn't have to wait long, though. The doctor soon entered the small room. When he noticed Hector, he reached out a hand, and the two men shook.

"I'm Chance Demetrios."

"Hector Garza."

After quizzing Samantha about the fall, about any pain she might be having, he suggested a sonogram, "Just as a precaution."

It took a while for them to set things up, and Hector couldn't help saying a silent prayer that the babies were all right, and that Samantha was, too.

As Dr. Demetrios scanned Samantha's belly, Hector focused on the grainy, black-and-white screen. He was amazed as the doctor pointed out the babies—little ones A, B and C.

Andrew, Brandon and Chloe, Hector thought to interject, but he bit his tongue.

As the doctor showed them the beating hearts, Hector was overwhelmed at the sight of those precious little babies, so vulnerable, so tiny. And his own stubborn heart melted.

"Everything looks good," the doctor said. "But I want you to go home and take it easy for a few days as a precaution. No heavy lifting, no stress. Do you have anyone who can stay with you and help out?"

"She has me," Hector said, knowing he was being sucked in again. But it didn't matter this time. His life and Samantha's were somehow connected.

When the doctor left the exam room, Hector helped Samantha down from the table. Then he escorted her out the door.

"I really appreciate this," she said. "You've been so good to me."

Because he loved her, he realized. But he didn't dare tell her here. So he waited until he drove her home and put her to bed.

"I'm going to stay the night," he told her, not expecting or willing to accept an objection. He refused to think about Peter, about what he and Samantha had once shared. At this point, it was more important that she was comfortable.

"Thanks, I'd appreciate that. I sleep better when you're with me."

He struggled not to take that as proof that she cared for him, that whatever secondary feelings she had for him would be enough.

But when she reached for his arm and gave it a squeeze that insisted he look at her, he found it impossible to pull away or completely shut her out.

When she had his attention, she said, "I love you, Hector."

His heart stood still. Was it enough? He wanted it to be.

"I loved Peter, too," she added. "But not in the same way."

"You don't have to say that," he said.

"Yes, I do. I need to be honest from here on out."

And so did he.

He took her hand. "Sam, I'm sorry that I was so hard on you the other day. I was angry and disappointed, but only because…I love you. And I'm… jealous of Peter."

Her eyes glistened. "You *love* me?"

"Yeah. I'm completely smitten. And even if I can't compete with Peter in your heart, I'm willing to give our relationship a try."

She smiled and patted a spot on the mattress beside her. And he took a seat.

"Don't be jealous of Peter," she said. "There will always be a place in my heart for him. He came into my life at a time when I didn't think I'd ever find a man I could trust. And he showed me a brand-new world. So how could I not love him? But what I felt for Peter," she continued, "and what I feel for you are two completely different things. You'll never have to compete with him in my heart, Hector. I love you in an entirely different way. A special way."

"You love me?" he asked, wanting to hear it again.

"More than I'd imagined." She scooted to the side and made room for him on the bed.

He kicked off his shoes and joined her, wrapping his arms around her and pulling her close.

"Those nights when you and I slept together," she said, "were the best I'd ever spent. In those hours just before dawn, we shared an intimacy I'd never experienced, not even with Peter. They were the most memorable nights I've ever had, and I realized that making love with you was going to be special."

Hector drew her close, resting his cheek against her hair. "I love you, Sam. And not just you. I love those babies, too. I want to be their father. And I'll honor

Peter's memory. I'll remember him as the man who took a broken young woman and provided her with the kind of life she deserved."

"You have no idea how happy I am to hear that," she said. "Or how much I love you."

"If it's anywhere near as much as I love you, then I have a pretty good handle on it."

She laughed. "Maybe you do."

"Marry me, Sam. Before the babies are born."

"Yes," she said, smiling. "Three times yes."

As he kissed her gently but thoroughly, something told him they were going to be three times happy.

* * * * *

Don't miss the next installment in the new Special Edition continuity, THE BABY CHASE

Billionaire Rourke Devlin wants children—badly—but he's not willing to risk his fortune on the wrong woman. The perfect solution? A marriage of convenience to Lisa Armstrong. It's only a matter of time before the business deal becomes a matter of the heart for these two! Look for
THE BILLIONAIRE'S BABY PLAN
By Allison Leigh
On sale June 2010,
wherever Silhouette Books are sold.

Kay Young returned to woozy consciousness to find that she was lying on a soft sofa beneath a heap of quilts near a cheerfully burning fire. When she tried to move, however, everything hurt, and she groaned.

At once she heard a sound, then a stranger with a hard, harsh face was squatting beside her. "Shh," he said softly. "You're safe here. I promise."

"I have to go," she said weakly, struggling against pain. "He'll find me. He can't find me."

"Easy, lady," he said quietly. "You're hurt. No one's going to find you here."

"He will," she said desperately, terror clutching at her insides. "He always finds me!"

"Easy," he said again. "There's a blizzard outside. No one's getting here tonight, not even the doctor. I know, because I tried."

"Doctor? I don't need a doctor! I've got to get away."

"There's nowhere to go tonight," he said levelly. "And if I thought you could stand, I'd take you to a window and show you."

But even as she tried once more to pull away the quilts, she remembered something else: this man had been gentle when he'd found her beside the road, even when she had kicked and clawed. He hadn't hurt her.

Terror receded just a bit. She looked at him and detected signs of true concern there.

The terror eased another notch and she let her head sag on the pillow. "He always finds me," she whispered.

"Not here. Not tonight. That much I can guarantee."

Will Kay's mysterious rescuer
protect her from her worst fears?
Find out in HER HERO IN HIDING by New York
Times *bestselling author Rachel Lee.*
Available June 2010,
only from Silhouette® Romantic Suspense.

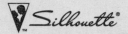

ROMANTIC
SUSPENSE

Sparked by Danger, Fueled by Passion.

NEW YORK TIMES AND *USA TODAY*
BESTSELLING AUTHOR

RACHEL LEE

BRINGS YOU AN ALL-NEW
CONARD COUNTY: THE NEXT GENERATION SAGA!

After finding the injured Kay Young on a deserted country
road Clint Ardmore learns that she is not only being hunted
by a serial killer, but is also three months pregnant.
He is determined to protect them—even if it means
forgoing the solitude that he has come to appreciate.
But will Clint grow fond of having an attractive woman
occupy his otherwise empty ranch?

Find out in

Her Hero in Hiding

Available June 2010 wherever books are sold.

Visit Silhouette Books at www.eHarlequin.com

SRS27681

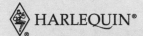

Harlequin® American Romance®

The Best Man in Texas
TANYA MICHAELS

Brooke Nichols—soon to be Brooke Baker—
hates surprises. Growing up in an unstable
environment, she's happy to be putting down
roots with her safe, steady fiancé. Then she meets
his best friend, Jake McBride, a firefighter and
former soldier who's raw, unpredictable and
passionate. With his spontaneous streak and
dangerous career, Jake is everything Brooke is
trying to avoid…so why is it so hard to resist him?

**Available June
wherever books are sold.**

"LOVE, HOME & HAPPINESS"

Silhouette Desire

From *USA TODAY* bestselling author

LEANNE BANKS

CEO'S EXPECTANT SECRETARY

Elle Linton is hiding more than just her affair
with her boss Brock Maddox. And she's
terrifed that if their secret turns public her
mother's life may be put at risk. When she
unexpectedly becomes pregnant she's forced
to make a decision. Will she be able to save
her relationship and her mother's life?

*Available June
wherever books are sold.*

Always Powerful, Passionate and Provocative.

HARLEQUIN *Romance*®

GIRLS' *Weekend in* VEGAS

Four friends, four dream weddings!

On a girly weekend in Las Vegas, best friends Alex, Molly, Serena and Jayne are supposed to just have fun and forget men, but they end up meeting their perfect matches! Will the love they find in Vegas stay in Vegas?

Find out in this sassy, fun and wildly romantic miniseries all about love and friendship!

═══════════

Saving Cinderella! by MYRNA MACKENZIE
Available June

Vegas Pregnancy Surprise by SHIRLEY JUMP
Available July

Inconveniently Wed! by JACKIE BRAUN
Available August

Wedding Date with the Best Man
by MELISSA MCCLONE
Available September

www.eHarlequin.com

HRI7663

HARLEQUIN

Ambassadors

Want to share your passion for reading Harlequin® Books?

Become a Harlequin Ambassador!

Harlequin Ambassadors are a group of passionate and well-connected readers who are willing to share their joy of reading Harlequin® books with family and friends.

You'll be sent all the tools you need to spark great conversation, including free books!

All we ask is that you share the romance with your friends and family!

You'll also be invited to have a say in new book ideas and exchange opinions with women just like you!

To see if you qualify* to be a Harlequin Ambassador, please visit www.HarlequinAmbassadors.com.

*Please note that not everyone who applies to be a Harlequin Ambassador will qualify. For more information please visit www.HarlequinAmbassadors.com.

Thank you for your participation.

BAP098PA

Love Inspired®

Bestselling author

JILLIAN HART

brings you another heartwarming story
from

the

GRANGER FAMILY RANCH

Rancher Justin Granger hasn't seen his high school sweetheart
since she rode out of town with his heart. Now she's back, with
sadness in her eyes, seeking a job as his cook and housekeeper.
He agrees but is determined to avoid her...until he discovers
that her big dream has always been him!

The Rancher's Promise

*Available June
wherever books are sold.*

Steeple
Hill®

LI87601

www.SteepleHill.com

REQUEST YOUR FREE BOOKS!
2 FREE NOVELS PLUS 2 FREE GIFTS!

SPECIAL EDITION
Life, Love and Family!

YES! Please send me 2 FREE Silhouette® Special Edition® novels and my 2 FREE gifts (gifts are worth about $10). After receiving them, if I don't wish to receive any more books, I can return the shipping statement marked "cancel." If I don't cancel, I will receive 6 brand-new novels every month and be billed just $4.24 per book in the U.S. or $4.99 per book in Canada. That's a saving of 15% off the cover price! It's quite a bargain! Shipping and handling is just 50¢ per book.* I understand that accepting the 2 free books and gifts places me under no obligation to buy anything. I can always return a shipment and cancel at any time. Even if I never buy another book from Silhouette, the two free books and gifts are mine to keep forever.

235/335 SDN E5RG

Name	(PLEASE PRINT)	
Address		Apt. #
City	State/Prov.	Zip/Postal Code

Signature (if under 18, a parent or guardian must sign)

Mail to the Silhouette Reader Service:
IN U.S.A.: P.O. Box 1867, Buffalo, NY 14240-1867
IN CANADA: P.O. Box 609, Fort Erie, Ontario L2A 5X3

Not valid for current subscribers to Silhouette Special Edition books.

Want to try two free books from another line?
Call 1-800-873-8635 or visit www.morefreebooks.com.

* Terms and prices subject to change without notice. Prices do not include applicable taxes. N.Y. residents add applicable sales tax. Canadian residents will be charged applicable provincial taxes and GST. Offer not valid in Quebec. This offer is limited to one order per household. All orders subject to approval. Credit or debit balances in a customer's account(s) may be offset by any other outstanding balance owed by or to the customer. Please allow 4 to 6 weeks for delivery. Offer available while quantities last.

Your Privacy: Silhouette is committed to protecting your privacy. Our Privacy Policy is available online at www.eHarlequin.com or upon request from the Reader Service. From time to time we make our lists of customers available to reputable third parties who may have a product or service of interest to you. If you would prefer we not share your name and address, please check here. ☐

Help us get it right—We strive for accurate, respectful and relevant communications. To clarify or modify your communication preferences, visit us at www.ReaderService.com/consumerchoice.